the
Elephant
in the
Room

ALSO BY HOLLY GOLDBERG SLOAN

Appleblossom the Possum

Counting by 7s

I'll Be There

Just Call My Name

Short

To Night Owl from Dogfish
(with Meg Wolitzer)

the Elephant in the Room

HOLLY GOLDBERG SLOAN

Dial Books for Young Readers

Dial Books for Young Readers
An imprint of Penguin Random House LLC, New York

First published in the United States of America by Dial Books for Young Readers, 2021
First paperback edition published 2022

THE LIBRARY OF CONGRESS HAS CATALOGED THE HARDCOVER EDITION AS FOLLOWS:
Names: Sloan, Holly Goldberg, date, author.
Title: The elephant in the room / Holly Goldberg Sloan.
Description: New York : Dial Books for Young Readers, 2021. | Audience: Ages 10 and up. | Audience: Grades 4 and up. | Summary: Missing her mother, who has returned to Turkey to resolve an immigration problem, sixth grader Sila welcomes a very large distraction in her life when she helps a surprising new friend rescue a circus elephant.
Identifiers: LCCN 2020049193 (print) | LCCN 2020049194 (ebook) |
ISBN 9780735229945 (hardcover) | ISBN 9780735229969 (ebook)
Subjects: CYAC: Friendship—Fiction. | Elephants—Fiction. | Separation (Psychology)—Fiction. | Emigration and immigration—Fiction. | Turkish Americans—Fiction.
Classification: LCC PZ7.S633136 El 2021 (print) | LCC PZ7.S633136 (ebook) | DDC [Fic]—dc23
LC record available at https://lccn.loc.gov/2020049193
LC ebook record available at https://lccn.loc.gov/2020049194

Book manufactured in Canada

ISBN 9780735229952

10 9 8 7 6 5 4 3 2 1

FRI

Design by Mina Chung • Text set in Diverda Serif

For Rae,
Abe, Sam,
and Harlan

the Elephant in the Room

1.

What Sila Tekin would remember about that afternoon was that she had been wearing her favorite shirt. It was nothing fancy. Just red with white stripes and blue stitching, but it fit perfectly, not too tight and not too loose. And it wasn't only comfortable; it was lucky, because she had been wearing the shirt when she found a twenty-dollar bill on the sidewalk one afternoon while walking home from school. Sila had also bowled her highest score in August, and done well on a very hard math test while wearing the garment. Another time when she had on the shirt she'd spotted a two-foot-tall speckled owl sleeping high up in a tree in Hendricks Park. That was amazing.

So the T-shirt was special. There was no question about it.

At least not until Thursday, September 6, when Sila came through the front door of the apartment to find her parents in the kitchen. Her mom and dad were never there when she got home from school; they were always at work. Her mom's eyes were red and puffy from crying and her nose

looked like it was leaking water. Sila asked in Turkish, which was the language she spoke at home, "What's going on?"

Her father put his hand on his daughter's shoulder. She could feel tension even in his fingertips. "We've had some bad news."

Sila's ears started to buzz. One of her grandparents must have died. Her voice was shaky as she asked: "What's happened? You have to tell me!"

Sila's mother, Oya, looked as if she was going to speak, only nothing came out except a long, dry exhale that had choking sounds mixed in. But then her father managed, "Your mother is going on a trip. She'll be back soon. Very soon."

"A trip? Why?"

"Legal things. Fixing paperwork."

Sila looked at her mother. "Where are you going?"

"To Turkey."

Sila's eyes moved from her mother to her father. They weren't sick. No one had died. Health wasn't the issue. Sila stared at her parents and could see they were trying to seem calm, but it looked as if their heads were going to explode.

"I don't understand. So what's the bad news?"

Her mother wiped her nose. "It's immigration. There is a problem."

Sila's parents went on to explain that Oya needed to return to the country she left as an adult and get a replacement for a document that had never been properly executed. Without fixing the situation, Oya was facing a court proceeding and even deportation. So she just needed to correct a clerical mistake. They had a plan.

It didn't sound to Sila like that big of a deal. Hadn't her mother admitted she missed where she was born? Couldn't going back to Turkey be a good thing? Didn't Oya speak all the time about longing to see Sila's grandparents? Wasn't she always saying she missed the bread and the cheese and the tomatoes she'd grown up with?

But this trip was forced on her. Maybe, Sila thought, anything that you are told to do isn't as good as when you make the choice yourself.

Everyone wants to be the boss of their own life.

Sila had been born in Oregon. She was an American citizen. Her parents had lived in Eugene for almost fifteen years, but they were Turkish citizens. In Istanbul her mother had studied to be a librarian, but once they came to America she had taken work in the housekeeping department of the most expensive hotel on main street. She cleaned rooms five days a week, and if she was lucky, got overtime for a sixth day. That job had ended after fourteen years only last week. So much was in turmoil.

These were the facts: Sila's mother would be gone for eight days—two Sundays with six days sandwiched in between. Before Oya left, she cooked her husband's and daughter's favorite foods and then packed the refrigerator and the freezer tight with glass containers. While her mother buzzed around the oven and the stove, Sila tried to be helpful and cleaned the apartment. When she was finished, she cleaned it all over again. She would have started on a third round but she went with her mother to shop for the gifts to bring for family and friends.

Later that night Sila sat on her parents' bed as Oya filled a large suitcase with wrapped presents. Once they were in place she had room for only three outfits, a week's worth of underwear, and four pairs of socks. Her mother insisted this would be enough for the short time she would be traveling.

Sila didn't think so, but said nothing.

Her parents took money from their savings and then more money from a credit card to finance the trip. Sila could see that her mom was nervous when she said goodbye. Oya pressed a blue glass evil eye on a chain into her daughter's

4

hand and told her to keep it with her at all times for protection. Sila didn't think her mother believed in curses, but she looked pretty serious. It was, she knew, bad luck to be superstitious.

Sila slipped the gold chain around her neck. She didn't want to cry. Her mother whispered, "Eight days will go by so fast. You'll see."

But the eight days had turned into eight months. Sila had hung a calendar on a wall in her room, and she put an X in the appropriate square every night before she went to bed. She then wrote the number of days her mother been gone. She was now on 237.

Sila loved her father, but being apart from her mom was harder than anything she had ever known. She missed her so much that even her skin didn't feel right. The air was pushing down on her arms in a new way and her feet somehow moved as if they were twice their former size.

At first Sila's dad, Alp, didn't eat much. He wore the same shirt for three days in a row, and wasn't shaving every morning. He spoke to his wife all the time, often trying to hide it from Sila. But she knew. She could hear her mother crying. On Skype. On the phone. Alp would be in the bedroom with the door shut, or even in the bathroom whispering as if Sila didn't have ears.

It took some time for them to get used to the fact that they were facing a crisis. It was sharp in the beginning and time turned it to something deep and dull and even more difficult. It turned into their new reality.

One of the hardest things was that Sila kept expecting to see her mother everywhere. When she came into the kitchen she looked for her at the stove. Her mom should have been on the couch. In the front seat of the car. Coming out of the bathroom. Her mother was there in Sila's head and her heart but not in the room.

And who knew when she would be coming back?

Waiting was what they did now.

Oya Tekin had flown to a place Sila had only heard about, but never seen. Her mother had gone back to Turkey. She had waited in lines. She had called officials. She had shown her file over and over and over again, and was told it was a process, which took time. Every day Sila and her father woke up hoping that the necessary paperwork was at the embassy in Ankara. But there was no answer to the biggest question: When would Oya get what she needed to fly back across the ocean and then across a continent to the place she called home?

In all the months that her mother had been gone, Sila had not once put on the red-and-white shirt with the blue stitching. The shirt had turned into a symbol for all the bad luck in the universe. Sila wanted to rip it apart and throw it away, but instead she stuffed the shirt into a plastic bag, which she jammed under the kitchen sink.

As the days and then weeks and then months passed, Sila stopped spending time with her friends. She came straight home every day after school and stayed in her room with her family's computer as a companion. Sila lost track of many of the things that she used to find fun, and clung to a very specific routine. She told no one about her situation. It wasn't anyone's business.

Sila did chores with her father on weekends, taking the laundry downstairs to the room off the parking garage on Saturdays. She vacuumed the apartment on Sundays, because that's what her mother had done.

She and Alp had stretched out her mother's home-cooked food for as long as possible, but it had been gone for months now. They tried to make meals the way they used to eat as a family, with vegetables, a salad, fish or chicken, and bread, but it was a lost cause. Mostly they ate scrambled eggs and toast for dinner.

Her father always read as he consumed his food. He worked as a car mechanic at an independent repair shop, and Sila was sure he was one of the few people in the world to find an owner's manual interesting. Sila just stared at the computer screen, keeping the sound on mute.

The best part of the day was when her mother would appear online at the arranged time. They talked. They laughed. They tried not to cry. They worked to keep it light-hearted. It was amazing how much they spoke about the weather. It was a neutral subject that was ever changing. But maybe more to the point, there was nothing they could do about it. Is that why talking about rain felt safe?

Because the time online was never enough. Once they had said goodbye the empty space would return. Sila and Alp didn't speak much to each other after the calls. Waiting made silence easier to tolerate than voices. No one but Sila's father understood, because no one else but him was feeling the same thing.

The rest of the world was getting on with their lives.

2.

The only expensive thing in Apartment 207A at 2599 Cleary Road was an intricately woven carpet that Sila's grandparents had shipped over from Istanbul. The Tekins' living space was home to geometrically patterned tiles and hand-painted Iznik ceramics, and then a lot of stuff from thrift stores and garage sales and discount stores. Sila once loved it all. Now it looked like a collection of things that didn't belong together.

Sila had her own bedroom, but other people living in the same units on other floors in the building used the space as an office because the area was tiny and had no closet. There was one round window in Sila's room, and it faced away from the street to the back, where railroad tracks were located. Sila had long ago grown so accustomed to the trains that she didn't hear them anymore. It was, she decided, like the way you don't see your own nose even though it's in your field of vision. Your brain says it's useless information.

But since her mother had gone, Sila could hear every single train that rattled past. She watched through the glass and imagined all the people traveling and felt her stomach knot. They all had somewhere to go.

It was a Saturday morning when Sila heard her father's cell phone ring. She watched as he wrote something on the back of an envelope and said, "I can be there in the next hour."

Sila moved from her spot on a stool and looked down at the address. She'd never heard of the street. "Dad, where's that?"

"Someplace out of town. Off old Route 99. You should come with me. I'm going out there to look at a truck that won't start."

"I'd rather stay here. I don't like trucks."

"And I don't like leaving you here alone for so long."

"Maybe you'll fix it in a few minutes and be right back."

"I'm not asking you to go. I'm—"

"Forcing me."

"Bring a book. It will be good for you to get out of the house."

"It's an apartment."

"We're leaving in twenty minutes."

Sila thought about putting up a fight but it wasn't worth it. For either of them. Her father would make her go in the end anyway, so Sila went to the kitchen and put water in the bottle she took to school every day. She then filled three plastic ziplock bags with hard cheese, sunflower seeds, and stale pretzels (someone hadn't shut the bag correctly, but since she and her father were both capable of that, she didn't say anything).

Sila stuffed the bags in her sweatshirt pocket. The last thing she did was retrieve a half-filled box of Junior Mints that she had been saving in her room. Her father could go forever fixing something and not need even a glass of water. They were different that way.

Twenty minutes later, Sila and Alp were driving out of town together on old Highway 99 North. It was surprising how good it felt to be moving. Sila wished they were going to travel like this for days with the radio on and the windows down heading across country until they reached the Atlantic Ocean. But even passing through twelve states and driving three thousand miles wouldn't make a difference. They would still be a whole body of salt water from the person who mattered most in their lives.

It wasn't very long before her father turned off the highway onto a narrow country road. There were no houses in sight, only fields with tall weeds that would come up past her knees. Sila wondered if there were snakes or rodents hiding in holes out in the meadows. She spotted what she thought was a hawk circling overhead and was curious what the bird saw that she couldn't.

Another five minutes passed, with only one other car going the other direction, when Sila's dad turned onto a gravel drive. As they rounded a bend they could see a very high wall made of big rocks. It looked to Sila like something that would surround a castle. There were huge wooden gates that went across a driveway and connected to the stone barrier. This, according to the address on the piece of paper Sila's father held in his hand, was where they were going. He stared at the wall. "Now, that took a lot of work."

"It looks so old."

"It's beautiful—no?"

"The wall goes on forever."

"Probably not forever. But yes, as far as we can see."

Sila felt a strange excitement as they approached. This place was filled with intrigue. Maybe they'd be here for hours and hours and hours. Maybe even days. But then dread took hold. That was the pattern now. What if her mother came home and no one was there? Being away from the apartment suddenly felt disloyal.

They weren't standing guard in the living room waiting for her.

They weren't near the computer.

They were out in the world.

Was there even good cell phone service this far out of town?

Who knew what could happen?

3.

Alp pushed a button on a call box next to the wooden gates. Right away they heard sharp chirping sounds coming from the trees. Out the windshield Sila could see a small flock of red finches against the gray Oregon sky. The sight of the little birds felt hopeful.

Her father's focus was on the intercom. He pressed the button on the box again, and a voice finally said: "Hello . . ."

"It's Alp Tekin. I've come about your truck."

A buzzer sounded and then the wooden gates started to roll open. Sila noticed that they had sturdy metal wheels on the bottom and big, dark metal hinges. Alp drove forward, and up ahead they could see a large, old pink farmhouse, a weathered barn, and an ancient-looking windmill that probably pumped water at one time but was now a lasting monument to a different era. Sila noticed that the front porch was surrounded by interesting overgrown plants. A lot of them were exotic, not like stuff that she'd seen wild in Oregon. "I didn't know you could grow palm trees here . . ."

Alp stared at the sago palms. They were tucked around one side of the farmhouse as if drawing warmth from the building. "Me neither."

"How come the plants don't die when it snows?"

He must not have known the answer, because he said, "Where your mom and I grew up in Turkey, there were places with palm trees."

"Yeah, but you guys love pine trees. I think palms are better."

"Is something better because you don't see it all the time?"

When her dad offered up his ideas they usually came out as questions.

Maybe her mother right now was sitting in a grove of palm trees. Sila saw that image in her mind's eye. It was strangely comforting.

The door to the pink farmhouse opened and an old man came out. He had mostly gray hair, a full white beard, and he was wearing a lemon-yellow jacket. Sila tried to remember if she'd ever seen her father in a yellow jacket. It was possible that he had a raincoat that color. The boys at her school must have thought that bright colors were only for highway workers, because almost everything they wore was blue, gray, brown, or black. Sila looked over at her dad. He had on jeans and a gray shirt. It was as if there were some kind of secret dress code they were all following, she thought. But not this old guy.

Sila's dad leaned out the open window on his side of the car. "I brought my daughter. This is Sila. I hope that's okay."

Sila had been taught that it was important to make a good first impression. It was also (according to her mom, who had made a lot of the rules) necessary to make a good second, third, and fourth impression, which was another way to say that her daughter needed to have good manners all the time. Sila tried to smile, but the corners of her mouth had lost whatever natural will they once possessed to turn upward. At least her teeth didn't stick to her lips. She'd been eating pretzels and her mouth felt salty and dry.

The older man spoke in a voice that Sila thought sounded like gravel. It was rocky like the road to his farmhouse and there was crunch in his words.

"I'm Gio. Nice to meet you two. My truck's in the barn. Drove it in there to give it a break from the rain. The thing's got enough rust spots. Now I can't get it started. Should we go take a look?"

Many times when Alp went to fix a car or truck, it was on the side of the road, or stuck somewhere, like in the mud. He didn't mind working in the wet weather, but Sila thought the look on his face said he was glad that Gio's broken vehicle was under cover. It was late spring and in Oregon that meant that the sky could open up in a downpour at any moment that would last for hours.

Sila swallowed a few times to get rid of the pretzel pieces that were lodged around her mouth between her teeth. Her plan had been to stay in her father's car while he worked, but then she heard the old man's voice: "Are you coming with us?"

Sila looked up at him. She thought of all the excuses for why she was going to stay in the car and was surprised to hear herself say, "Okay. Sure."

Alp lifted his toolbox and they both followed Gio. Sila thought the old man moved pretty fast considering his right knee didn't bend in the same way as his left knee did. One of the rules when she went with her dad on work trips was to approach everyone she met not just with respect but also with caution. You shouldn't trust someone, she had been taught, until you really knew the person.

Gio pushed opened the barn's large double doors and

Sila and Alp followed him inside. An old blue pickup was parked in the middle of the cavernous space. Sila wondered if at one time the barn had housed pigs and cows and chickens. She also imagined ponies and geese and sheep. Instead there were just a lot of spiderwebs.

Alp went to work looking under the hood of the truck, and Sila was unsure if she should wait at his side or whether the old man expected her to talk to him. Then she heard, "I went to the bakery on Route 99 this morning. I have donuts. Would you like one?"

Sila sat on the front porch of the farmhouse and Gio brought out a plate with a jelly-filled cruller, a chocolate-glazed thug, and a large cinnamon twist. Sila took her time making her choice, but in the end she went for the cinnamon twist because it was the biggest thing on the plate and if her mouth was full she wouldn't be expected to talk.

Gio went back inside and returned minutes later with a cup of coffee for himself and a glass of milk for Sila. They ate donuts in silence until all three were gone. Sila was surprised she didn't feel uncomfortable. The man in the yellow jacket didn't seem to care about talking. It was a huge relief.

Sila's mother had said it wasn't good manners to stare at

your phone if you were with someone else, so Sila resisted the temptation. She drank what was left of the milk and watched the birds in the trees. Gio sipped his coffee. Finally Sila said, "So, did you build that stone wall?"

"I did not."

"The barn is so big. But you don't have any animals."

"I don't."

"Are you a farmer?"

"I was thinking of farming when I bought this place. But I haven't done that. I've only been out here for a few months."

Gio took another sip of his coffee and then he sat back and told her about the last eight months of his life.

4.

"For almost thirty years I worked as a carpenter, but then a place called Chinook Modular Housing opened up off River Road. You're too young to remember when all that land was a blueberry farm."

Sila nodded.

"Well, they plowed under the bushes and built an assembly plant. I took a job out there. We made housing units—Chinook mobile homes."

"How do you build a mobile home?"

"The things start as big metal skeletons that are shipped from China. Those pieces get welded together. After that, a wooden frame goes on, which was my part. Then plumbers and electricians come on board. Once that happened my crew would start all over again on another unit. For sixteen years I built the same thing, the same way, with the same materials, five days a week."

Sila took a moment to imagine what his job was like. "Was it boring?"

Gio laughed. "I could put the thing together with my eyes closed. Well, almost. It wasn't exciting. But I worked out of the rain. And it took some skill."

"Were you allowed to listen to music?"

"We did do that."

"Did you like the other people you worked with?"

"We were a good group. We had a bowling league and a book club. We needed things to talk about besides each other. We didn't want to spend too much time gossiping."

"My teacher last year said that gossip is telling stories that you don't know are true. But most of the stuff kids repeated was true. So does that make it gossip?"

"Hard to say. I think of gossip as being mean."

Sila managed a half smile. "I agree."

"Anyway, at one point a bunch of us at work decided to play the lottery."

Sila repeated the slogan she'd heard on local television commercials: "Powerball and Mega Millions. Hey! Somebody's gotta win."

"That's right. Our friend Corey was in charge. Twenty-four of us put in money and Corey bought tickets every week. It was too much trouble after a while picking all the numbers, so we used an online program that chose random ones, but we always used the number twenty-four. Because that was us. Twenty-four Chinook workers. Well, we played the lottery for six years, four months, and three days . . ."

Gio stopped to take a sip of his coffee. His eyes had lit up, and Sila realized she was holding her breath as she waited. He swallowed his coffee and continued, "When one wet, foggy Saturday—it was October twenty-fourth of this past year—we had the winning ticket."

Sila couldn't help but be excited. "You won!"

"We did."

"Was it a ton of money?"

"It was. Even split twenty-four ways. It was the largest jackpot in the state's history. No one had won for eighteen weeks. The prize kept rolling over, getting bigger and bigger."

"Did you freak out when you heard the news?"

"I didn't believe it at first. It felt like a dream. Or a crazy hoax or scam someone was playing on us. My friend Rosa called me crying. She worked in accounting. I thought her cat had died. She'd been really worried about that cat. But she was happy-crying."

"I guess it sounds the same."

"Especially when all you hear is someone having trouble breathing. It was a weekend and no one was at work, but we all jumped into cars and met in the Chinook parking lot. We were screaming and shaking and falling all over each other. Dee Dee Pratt even fainted. There are more than a hundred and fifty people who are employed out there, but we were the lucky ones. I can tell you for a fact that come Monday the other workers really weren't that happy for us."

"Maybe they felt left out."

"It was like someone died. They walked around with their heads down, trying to smile but really filled with grief. Even the president of the company, a guy named Ronnie Roberts, didn't come in for three days. That's how much it shook people up. And yes, of course they were mad that they weren't part of our lottery group."

Sila nodded. "I guess for once everyone at work was talking about the same thing."

It looked to Sila as if Gio was enjoying telling his story. She wondered if he'd spent the last eight months keeping what had happened private from anyone not directly involved. She felt no envy as she listened, and was happy when he continued, "Three weeks after the Big Saturday, all of us, except a welder named Duncan Maynard, had quit our jobs. Duncan said he really liked installing windows and he didn't care that he had a ton of money heading his way."

"I wonder if he got treated differently at work after that."

"I'm sure he did. The day we got the check we took a group photo in front of the Chinook Modular Housing sign. I've got it right here."

Gio pulled his phone from his coat pocket and scrolled to a picture. He held it up for Sila. She squinted at the screen.

"Which one is Duncan Maynard?"

Gio pointed to a man in the front. Sila looked carefully. "He's got the biggest smile."

Gio turned the phone back around. "You're right. I never noticed that. Most of us weren't getting a lot of sleep back then. We were still in shock."

"Well, he looks happy."

"He does. And he was the only one not going anywhere."

Gio put the phone back in his coat pocket and continued, "All I wanted that day was for my wife, Lillian, to be alive. She believed in playing the lottery more than I did. I've never been much of a gambler. But Lillian thought it was a fun thing to do. So she's the reason I was even part of it."

Sila's voice was small: "And she's not around now?"

"She passed away over four years ago."

Sila knew it wasn't polite to ask too many personal questions, but she wanted to know more. "What happened to her?"

"She was healthy until just after her sixty-first birthday when she got a sore shoulder. Then the pain moved to her back. We thought she'd pulled a muscle, or slept on her side funny. But it didn't go away. She wasn't someone who complained about stuff, so I forgot she even had a problem. After that, maybe a month later, she started to cough. It was winter and everyone was hacking away all the time. We just thought she had a bad cold."

Gio stopped abruptly and put down his coffee cup. When he started to speak again Sila heard the words spill out fast and dull. "She had lung cancer. She fought. It won."

"I'm sorry. . . ."

"Me too."

After a while Gio went back to talking. "So Lillian never knew I won the money. She worked hard her whole life, and she never got to see any of this. She always wanted to live on a farm. She liked to garden. She wanted a house with a second floor. She said she'd like a barn. That's why I'm here. It's for her."

Gio looked out onto the tall pines trees.

"Did you and your wife—"

"Lillian."

"Did you and Lillian have kids?"

"No. But she was always around young people. She taught second grade at Harriet Beecher Stowe Elementary School."

Sila's mouth opened and she looked wide-eyed at Gio. "Wait. What's your last name?"

"Gardino."

"So you were married to Mrs. Gardino?"

"I was."

"She was my second-grade teacher!"

"No kidding!"

"She was my favorite!"

Sila impulsively reached over and touched his hand. "I think about her all the time."

When she looked at Gio she realized his eyes were turning liquid.

5.

They heard the sound of an engine starting. Gio seemed to collect himself as the pickup truck emerged from the barn. "Your dad's got the old engine running again." Only moments later Alp cut the motor and got out of the vehicle.

"Your truck's working, but it won't stay that way. There's a problem with the alternator. It needs to be replaced, and then the fuel line should come out. I could have the parts shipped to me. That would take about ten days. If you're interested I can get you a price."

"You call and let me know what it will cost, but plan on doing it."

Sila looked at the old man in the lemon-yellow jacket and brightened. "So we'll have to come back."

She could see that Gio Gardino seemed to also feel as if not being able to fix the truck was some kind of good news. Gio took his checkbook out of his pocket and paid Alp, saying, "Sila, I enjoyed our chat. But I feel bad that I spent the whole time talking about myself."

"That's okay," Sila said.

"But I didn't learn enough about you. Except of course that you are a good listener."

Alp answered for her, "Sila likes books and animals."

Sila grumbled, "We're not allowed to have pets at our apartment, which is why we don't have a dog."

"What's your favorite animal?" Gio asked.

She answered immediately. "An elephant."

Gio laughed. "Well, I can see how you wouldn't be able to keep one of those in an apartment."

Sila smiled politely. Alp looked over at his daughter. Oya had made a stuffed elephant for Sila when she was very young, and more than eleven years later it was a lumpy gray mass with the button eyes long gone.

It still spent every night on Sila's bed.

Once they were in the car Sila told her father about Gio's lottery win.

"I remember that now. A big group of people. I heard one of them went into the Mercedes dealership on Franklin and bought four cars."

"Really?"

"I think it was the biggest lottery payout they've had."

"That's what he said. And guess what? His wife was my second-grade teacher. Mrs. Gardino. She was so nice."

"We'll have to tell your mother tonight. She'll remember her."

"She was my favorite teacher ever."

"And she's gone?"

Sila nodded. "She died four years ago. I guess I was in her last class. They didn't tell us much about what happened."

Alp glanced at his daughter. He tried to change the subject. "If I won the lottery I'd hire a great immigration lawyer. Maybe from someplace like New York City. Somebody who knew all the right people."

Sila's face scrunched up. "Is that the problem? We can't get Mom the visa because we know the wrong people?"

"The rules changed. That's a bigger problem. But still, it would help if we had a real advocate on our side."

"Dad, if we won the lottery, after we hired the right lawyer, I'd fix the sidewalk in front of our apartment. People trip out there all the time."

"I like that idea, Sila. It's very thoughtful."

"Thank you."

"What else would you do, little one?"

"I'd rent the apartment next door to us and make a door

connecting the two units. Then I'd have a big bedroom and also my own kitchen."

This made her father laugh. "So we'd have two kitchens to make eggs and toast."

"Exactly. But Mom would be back, so things would be normal and she'd like the extra oven for baking."

"Well, if I had some of that Powerball money I'd start my own auto mechanic business. I wouldn't work at the repair shop anymore or take weekend jobs."

They drove in silence for the next ten minutes, both thinking about the fantasy Powerball money they had. Sila finally spoke again as they pulled into their parking space at the apartment building. "I bet everyone who meets Gio starts thinking about all that money and what they'd do with it."

"No doubt."

"Maybe," she said, "that's why he moved out of town to live behind the big wall."

After Sila and Alp left, Gio sat in the chair in his living room where he had a good view of a photo of Lillian he had positioned at eye level on the bookcase. So his wife knew

Sila Tekin. It was such a small world. Lillian always spoke about the kids she taught, and Gio wished now that he could remember more of those conversations. Was he imagining that Lillian had spoken about the girl? He really couldn't be sure. But he guessed yes.

Gio knew one thing was for certain: If Lillian were still alive she would have gotten to the bottom of why Sila seemed sad. Instead, Gio now felt he shouldn't have spent so much time telling his story, even if it did seem to interest her. He looked out the window at the changing light on the distant hills, his two thousand acres that backed up against Flynn's Butte. He thought the low mountains looked like pillows. When he closed the deal on the property, the grass in between the tall trees was yellow, and at the end of the day the slopes turned gold. It was the land he loved, but also the old wooden farmhouse dating back almost one hundred years. It had been painted so many times that the color was speckled and from a distance appeared pink. To Gio it was weathered and worn, not peeling and shedding its skin. The structure with its steep roof, round windows, and large wraparound porch was unusual and filled with intrigue. A very old, green copper rooster weather vane perched at the highest point of the tallest gable. It spun around in a strong wind and the rusty bearings made a screeching sound as if the rooster were alive.

But what really set the property apart was that most of the acreage was enclosed by a high stone wall. This was what no one else had been willing to pay for.

Eighty years before, the owners of these hills had been in the quarry business, supplying gravel for the roads that early lumber companies had needed when they forged into the forests to cut down timber. The wall had started when the family decided to grow exotic plants and rare orchids. The climate was a problem, but the bigger issue was the deer that roamed the area. The animals went crazy for the new vegetation. A barrier needed to be put up, but the deer could jump, and so the wall was made higher and then higher, until it finally towered eight feet tall. The cost wasn't a problem for the family since the rock was free from their quarry, and the wall continued to be built, even after their interest in exotic plants faded.

No one had a wall like this wall. No one wanted one. But at a certain point the wall became a source of pride. The wall started for a specific reason. Then it became a hobby. And it ended as an obsession. The family couldn't stop themselves from more and more construction. Neighbors reported seeing people mixing cement and lifting boulders in the middle of the night. The result was that acres and acres of Gio's property were enclosed.

Local people wondered what the previous owners were doing on the other side of the high barrier, and stories were whispered about ghosts, secret ceremonies, and even illegal activity. Gio didn't pay attention. He loved the old farmhouse, the gentle slope of the hills, and the sound of the wind as it stirred the tops of the pine trees. The useless wall was something he was willing to accept because it was part of the package.

There was very little flat land available on Gio's new property and the whole place was dotted with trees. Enormous boulders seemed to pop up unexpectedly like huge eggs dropped from the sky. The earth hiding beneath the moss, ferns, and wildflowers was streaked with dense orange clay. It was not meant to grow vegetables. His plan to plant lettuce and tomatoes was permanently on hold.

Gio wasn't hiding out at the new place, but something close to that happened. Walls do that. They separate worlds. The winter months in the valley in this part of Oregon are wet, which means a lot of gray, closed-in skies. Gio started to believe he'd come to the end of the road in life. He wasn't an ancient man, but he was approaching his seventieth birthday. It felt like a lot of living, especially when his knees hurt and his back was sore every morning. Because his job had been in construction, his life had been very physical. He'd been a human pretzel, bent over while pounding nails or standing tall as he held wooden beams high over his head. Now he was a lottery winner with no money worries, no wife, an achy body, and a lot of time on his hands. The excitement of having a big bank account had worn off. There was no one waiting for him to show up at a job—no one expecting him to share a meal, or to even talk with about what to watch on TV. Gio was in a hole that can appear when a person doesn't feel they're needed.

He was no more happy, and no less happy, than before he won all the lottery money. But he was a whole lot more alone. He carried around an emptiness that was the space Lillian once filled. Missing her every day was the connection they now shared, and that meant she was still alive. He was seeing the world for both of them now. His steps were hers.

Had the little girl he'd met today lost someone?

Gio wondered if that was the look he saw in her eyes.

He wished he'd found a way to ask.

6.

Gio climbed inside his new truck the next afternoon and his vehicle seemed to drive itself into town, to the address listed on Alp Tekin's business card. He sat in front of 2599 Cleary Road and stared at the apartment building. Why was he there?

Gio watched as Alp Tekin's car came down the street. Sila was seated inside with her father. She spotted Gio before he could start his engine and drive off. This left him no choice but to roll down the window and come up with an explanation. "I brought you the money—so that you could order the parts for my old truck."

Alp nodded and said, "But it was okay to pay when I came back."

Gio opened the door to his vehicle and reached into his pocket, taking out a handful of hundred-dollar bills. Alp accepted the money, saying thank you, but what followed was an awkward pause, which Sila finally filled.

"Do you want to come in and have a cup of tea with us? Or maybe some cheese and olives?"

Gio surprised himself and them when he said, "Sure. That would be nice."

Sila put out a plate of snacks. Alp made tea and served it in little tulip-shaped, clear glasses with two lumps of sugar on the side. Gio sat at the table in the small kitchen. For once Sila was glad that her mom wasn't there; Oya always insisted people take off their shoes at the door. Alp and Sila hadn't said anything to Gio, who was wearing what looked like fancy leather bedroom slippers. Sila wondered if he'd forgotten to put on real shoes when he left home.

It had been quiet for what felt like a long time when Alp asked, "How did you end up calling me to fix your truck?"

Gio took a sip of tea and explained, "When my truck wouldn't start I thought about having it towed to the dealership in town. But then I remembered how they'd treated me the last time I came in. The head of the service department flat out said he didn't think the truck was worth repairing. I wasn't going near that pinched-face man again."

This made Alp laugh. Gio then continued: "I keep a stack of business cards in the kitchen. People offering up gardening services, housecleaning, and pet sitting—mostly stuff I don't need. When I lived in town, I'd get the cards put in the mailbox."

Sila's and Alp's eyes met and they both smiled. They sometimes walked together around town and left Alp's business cards in people's mailboxes. It always felt great to see that the work paid off.

"When I moved out to my new place I took the cards with me," Gio went on. "It's an old-fashioned way to look for employment, what with the Internet and all. I admire the effort."

Sila reached for one of the cards from a bowl on the kitchen counter. There was a small drawing of an elephant sitting in a wagon on Alp's business card. Sila told Gio, "I helped make the card. There's a program online and you just put in your information. I picked out the logo."

Talking about the business card made Gio come to life. He explained that while he'd bought a new truck with his lottery money, it was his old truck that he owned when his wife was still alive that he cared the most about.

"The upholstery in the front seat's split down the middle and there's yellowy sponge poking out. The floor mats are worn through and the outside paint long ago got dull. The truck has rust spots on the fenders and the hood. But it feels more comfortable than my new one—with its dashboard all lit up and the crazy warning sounds telling me to brake or stay in my lane when I know I'm doing just fine."

Alp nodded with understanding. Sila didn't care much about cars or trucks, but she liked this guy. He was making it feel less sad in the apartment.

"I put a battery in the old truck three months ago," Gio said. "So when I went out to drive it Saturday and it wouldn't start, I was surprised how rotten it made me feel. Things can just be moving one minute and not working the next."

Sila wondered if he was talking about the truck or himself. This man was one of the winners of the biggest lottery payout in the state, yet he had his problems. Everyone did. Since her mom had gone, Sila understood that.

Alp got up to put the teakettle back on the stove, and Gio looked at Alp's daughter. "What are you thinking about right now, Sila?" he asked.

She didn't take even a moment to answer. "Having my mom come home."

Gio nodded.

So there it was. The problem.

He'd known there was something forming a cloud over the girl.

And with that, the conversation changed to an explanation by Alp of new laws that required new documentation for immigrants, which was the reason they were waiting so anxiously at 2599 Cleary Road.

7.

Gio had let it slip out that the next day was his birthday. Sila hoped he wasn't going to be spending it alone. He had seemed vague when she asked, so they had made a plan. They would meet in the morning before school for donuts at Gio's favorite breakfast spot: the Hole in One bakery. He had explained to them, "It's really not a bakery because they only sell donuts. It's run by two sisters, Margo and Mayo. They don't keep regular hours and they sell whatever they've made, then close for the day."

Alp knew the Hole in One but had never been inside. "They have that huge parking lot," Gio said. "I think they lose money making donuts, but they hold a flea market on the property once a month. Truckers know the place because it's so easy to park."

That night Sila looked it up online. A review said: "Not far off the highway you can get a decent dunker and park ANYTHING there."

It was raining and windy outside when Sila and her father walked in to find the lottery winner staring into the glass case at the maple bars. It smelled like cinnamon and sugar, and Sila wondered if it was possible to make a perfume with the odor of a donut shop. She could imagine it being a best seller.

Gio had brought three coffee mugs from home. At the Hole in One they gave ten cents off for bringing in your own drink container. Gio said he was doing it to help the planet, not to save thirty cents. He and Alp ordered coffee. Sila asked for hot chocolate. They each picked out donuts.

Sila had made Gio a birthday card and she gave it to him while Alp paid the cashier. Gio read out loud what Sila had written inside: "May this be your best year yet." He thanked her, and she thought he looked genuinely happy as he slipped the card in the pocket of his yellow jacket.

They had just found seats by the window when three very large trucks pulled into the oversized parking lot. Two of the three were the kind of transporters that could carry very heavy loads. Both of these vehicles had been customized with a foot of open metal grating at the top on three of the four sides. These openings appeared to be designed to let in air. But why?

An old school bus, painted purple and green, motored into the lot behind the trucks. The bus was followed by two dented passenger vans, three SUVs, and five packed pickup trucks.

Behind the counter Margo could be heard grumbling, "Prepare for an invasion."

Sila was no longer fixated on her hot chocolate or cream-filled donut. She stared out the window. The rain was coming down hard as the doors to the vehicles opened and people started to spill out. Lots of people. Gio caught Sila's eye. "This could be interesting."

They weren't disappointed. The new arrivals were a lively bunch, dressed in bright clothing, with imaginative hairstyles, arms of tattoos, and rattling metal jewelry. A disproportionate number of the crowd wore hats and carried overflowing shoulder bags. Six poodles, dyed purple and pink, came out of one of the vans. In several minutes more than fifty people were waiting to use the donut shop bathroom. Those who didn't take a place in the crooked line headed to the glass counter and eyed the pastry with real enthusiasm. The group was loud. They talked and horsed around in a way that Sila decided meant many of them had to be related. It wasn't long before they were moving chairs, sitting in clusters, or standing to argue, while eating donuts and gulping coffee.

Sila was eager to know more about the group when a man close to Gio's age, with tangled long curls of silver hair, came over and pointed to an empty chair. He asked, "Anyone sitting here?" Gio responded, "It's reserved for you."

The man lowered himself down with obvious relief onto the red cushion of the metal chair. Sila tried not to eyeball the guy, but it was impossible. The newly arrived traveler had silver rings on all of his fingers, even his thumbs. He wore an orange scarf around his neck, a green army jacket, and faded striped pants, which were tucked into old yellow rain boots.

Sila wanted to say something and was grateful when Gio did it for her by asking, "Where's your group headed?"

The man took a big bite of his cinnamon twist and answered with his mouth full: "Nowhere. Real fast." The man swallowed. "Just finished our last booking."

Sila stared back out the window at the vehicles. She read the faded words painted on the side of one of the trucks: THE BRIOT FAMILY CIRCUS. She found herself asking, "So you're all in a circus?"

For the next fifteen minutes they heard that the Briot

family (along with some non-Briot employees) had traveled the country for almost thirty-two years. But while Chester Briot said he would like to keep moving from town to town entertaining small communities (never big cities—they weren't intended for that kind of crowd), his employees, who were his children, cousins, two former wives, and other stakeholders in the operation, had different ideas.

In Klamath Falls, the Briot circus members had taken a vote. As the ringmaster, Chester insisted that his single ballot count for ten, but even that hadn't made a difference. They'd come to the decision to stop performing at the end of the month, sell off what they could, and each go their own way. So they were, as Chester said, "getting ready to close down the big top for good."

Sila hadn't taken a single bite of her donut since the man opened his mouth. Gio saw the look on her face, a mixture of fascination and intrigue, and he went to the cash register and paid the bill for the whole group. It was donuts and coffee on Giovanni Gardino! This act of generosity, and the fact that Sila explained it was Gio's birthday, led Chester to invite Sila, Alp, and Gio out to meet another longtime member of the Briot circus.

The rain had tapered off to a sprinkle and the sun was poking through a hole in the thick clouds as the group followed the circus man out the door of the donut shop and into the large parking lot. A rainbow suddenly appeared in the sky. It formed an arch high above their heads that felt to Sila like destiny as Chester opened the back of the largest truck.

Because that's when Sila met Veda.

8.

Veda was an elegant elephant. She had dark brown eyes and long lashes that looked like they were made of black wire. In the tight space of the transport trailer she angled her head so that one eye could get a look back. Her gaze was penetrating. When their eyes connected Sila took in a big gulp of air. She was awestruck.

"I've never seen an animal this big."

Chester seemed to puff up with pride. "I got her when she was young. She was a lot smaller then. I've had her for years and years."

"Is it okay if I touch her?"

"Sure. Go ahead."

Sila reached up and her fingers brushed gently against the leathery gray hide of Veda's right back leg.

"She's amazing" was all Sila could manage to say.

Chester saw Sila staring in awe at his pachyderm. He'd long ago forgotten how majestic the elephant was. The cost of feeding and transporting the huge animal was worth it when the money was coming in, but that was back when crowds were waiting to greet the circus. Those days Chester was younger and life on the road with his family was an adventure.

He listened as the girl spoke, straining to hear her barely audible words. "There are two kinds of elephants. African and Asian. Like cousins, branches of the same family. The Asian elephants are smaller. They have different ears. An elephant is the second-smartest land animal. We come in first. We're mammals. We're related. But of course it's important to remember that all living things are related. I did a report on elephants at school last year."

Chester found himself saying with real feeling what he'd mouthed thousands of times into a microphone without much genuine emotion. "Elephants are inspiring. Just in size alone. They're the largest living land animals on the planet. They have twenty-six teeth. Tusks are teeth—did you all know that? They're incisors. But only male elephants have them. Veda's a female, so no tusks on her. An elephant can stand almost perfectly still for hours and hours. They use up almost no energy. Sounds crazy, but it's true. It's how they're built—where the bones are and all! Elephants get most of their sleep standing up. Bet you didn't know that."

Sila met his gaze. "I knew."

Alp shrugged. "I didn't."

Gio was silent.

Gio could tell that Sila would have spent the day standing there in the drizzle watching the enormous animal, but she had school. Her father gently reminded her that they needed to get going.

"But . . ."

"You have to get to class and I have to be at work."

Gio watched as Sila's eyes filled. She put her head down but managed to say "Happy birthday, Mr. Gardino."

"Gio."

Alp placed his hand on Sila's shoulder. "Yes. Happy birthday, Gio."

"Thank you. Both of you," he answered. "I won't forget this birthday."

Gio watched as Sila headed to Alp's car. Chester continued talking about the circus, but Gio wasn't listening to his words. He felt his stomach twist as his mind fixated on a single thought: He would never get over the look on Sila's face as she stared at the elephant. Gio had to place his left hand on the side of the circus truck to steady himself as he watched Sila and Alp's car recede down the highway.

Suddenly something shifted inside him, and he felt a kind of steadiness take hold that had been missing since Lillian died. Maybe his whole life had led to this. A man with not much to do but a ton of money meets an elephant that has been riding around in a truck for years.

Trapped.

Alone.

Wasn't this a perfect match?

This had to be the reason he'd won 1/24 of the Powerball millions! This had to be why he'd bought acres and acres of land surrounded by a ridiculously high stone wall! This had to be why he'd kept a mechanic's business card with an elephant logo for three years in a brass bowl and then moved it with his belongings to the farmhouse. This was why Sila and her father had shown up to fix the old truck.

Chester was still speaking and Gio heard him say, "The guy I bought her from named her. We tried to call her Jumba—get it? Not Jumbo. But she never took to it. So we went back to Veda."

Gio's voice was filled with anxiety as he asked, "What's your plan? You said you were closing down the circus. What will you do with your elephant?"

What Chester didn't explain when he talked about the problems of running a small, family-owned traveling show was that new laws affecting his work had been passed. Regulations had been put in place all across the country to stop performers from using tools to control circus animals. Those new rules were changing everything for people like Chester. He and his circus believed that they were kind enough to the four-legged members of the troupe, but they still needed a metal hook and electric prods or whips when running their show. And that was now against the law.

Suddenly it was as if the circus owner was seeing Gio for the first time. He didn't look like any kind of wealthy man, but this guy had just paid for a room full of strangers to have eighty-three donuts, forty-five hot drinks, and thirty-one bottles of water. That had never happened before. It had to mean something.

Chester glanced down at Gio's shoes. What a person wore on his feet was a clue to the size of his bank account. Chester flashed on his own rain boots, which were almost worthless. They just proved his point. The man standing next to him had on what appeared to be new, fine leather bedroom slippers. And he was wearing them outside of the house in the rain! That must mean that the old man had money and didn't care about wrecking perfectly good footwear.

There was no way Chester could know that Gio had a bunion on the joint below his right big toe and the slippers provided a measure of comfort he thought he couldn't find in other footwear. But he was right about one thing: It took money to purchase ten pairs of the fancy leather slippers, and these days Gio wore them inside and outside the house. Once they got too dirty, he tossed them in the trash. Lillian wasn't around to tell him that it was wasteful. He was careful with his money, but the slippers and Bing cherries out of season were two of his very few lottery-winning luxuries.

Margo and Mayo's Hole in One bakery wasn't the kind of eatery to find a *traditionally* wealthy man, but Chester Briot took the fancy bedroom slippers to be a good sign. This might be the place to find an eccentric old man with a lot of money. Was the guy a lumber baron? Or had he invented one of the first computer programs? This was the Pacific Northwest, after all. Hadn't Bill Gates come from the neighboring state? Or could the man in the slippers have once been a famous rock star? Did he write the song "Stairway to Heaven"? Somebody did.

Chester shut his eyes for the briefest of moments and imagined all of his toes and fingers crossing for good luck. He then said, "I don't want to part with Veda, but for a reasonable price, seeing as how we're closing down the operation, I guess I'd *consider* selling her. Elephants are very, very, very special. But also expensive. Would you know someone who might be interested?"

9

Sila had trouble concentrating. She could think of nothing except the elephant. But when she received a note only an hour after arriving at school directing her to go to the office, she snapped back to reality. Her mind raced as she walked down the empty corridor.

Being sent to the office could never be good news. Something bad must have happened. Did her father get in an accident? He worked underneath cars all day. What if one of the hydraulic lifts broke and he got hurt? Or was this about her mother?

She was all sweaty as she approached the front desk. "My name is Sila Tekin. I got a note to come in."

The woman behind the counter motioned toward a corner office. A sign next to the door said: MRS. HOLSING: ASSESSMENT AND CURRICULUM PROGRAMS COORDINATOR. Sila entered the room to find a woman seated on an exercise ball behind a desk. There was something about seeing an authority figure balancing on a big yellow ball that eased the tension. The

woman put her hand over the mouthpiece of a phone and said, "Sila, have a seat. I'm Joann Holsing."

Then she went back to talking, wrapping up the conversation with a lot of "Uh-huh. Yes. I see your point. Uh-huh. Yes."

Sila slid into a chair. Her eyes took in the room. The walls had been painted in the school colors, which were purple and white. It felt to Sila like they'd work better in a bedroom. Or a candy shop. On the desk in front of her was a computer. Three framed photos of a family. A stack of papers. And a collection of carved wooden animals. Sila's gaze stayed on the animals. She wondered if Mrs. Holsing was an animal person. Or maybe it was just that the woman knew somebody who liked to carve wood.

Sila's thoughts were interrupted.

"Miss Tekin, it's been brought to my attention that you are quiet in the classroom when you used to be a big contributor. You aren't doing as well in your studies as you have in the past. And it's also been reported that you eat lunch alone these days."

This hardly felt to Sila like a crime. She found herself wondering who did the "reporting." Her teachers had repeatedly asked her if there was a problem. Hadn't Sila dodged their concern? They wondered why she couldn't concentrate and she had no answer to give them. The emptiness was everywhere. But the school year was nearly over. Why bother with her now?

Mrs. Holsing leaned forward. "Is everything okay with you at home?"

Sila swallowed. Nothing was okay at home. Her mother was trapped overseas unable to return because her visa was no longer valid and because someone saw her as some kind of threat.

"Do you want to tell me about it?"

Sila shook her head.

"Is someone bullying you? Are you feeling threatened or intimidated or fearful?"

Sila was at this very moment feeling threatened, intimidated, and fearful. But she shook her head again.

They sat for a while longer in silence.

Then the woman shifted on the exercise ball and clicked her computer mouse and the screen changed. Sila wished she could see what it was the woman was looking at, but she was sitting at a bad angle.

"Okay, we want to put you in a pilot program. The state board of education is testing this in four schools, and we've been chosen. It's an honor. The concept is called 'Pairing.' One student is matched with another student who may or may not be feeling a similar level of social isolation."

Sila found her voice. "Social isolation?"

Mrs. Holsing was reading now from a set of questions on the screen: "When was the last time you made a new friend?"

Sila was surprised how easy it was to answer. "Just this past weekend."

"Really? That's wonderful. Tell me about the person."

"I met a guy who lives out of town on a big property. He's very nice."

"A man?"

"He's old. Like a grandpa."

"And he's a new friend?"

"Yes. Definitely. I knew his wife."

Sila stopped. She didn't want to explain about her old teacher. It felt as if that might make her cry.

"Okay. And when did you last see this new friend?"

"We had donuts just this morning. Before school. With my dad. It was his birthday and we saw—"

Mrs. Holsing cut her off. "What I was speaking about, in terms of friendship, was someone your own age."

"Oh."

They sat in silence again. Then finally: "Is it safe to say that you have not made a new friend your own age in quite a while?"

No answer from Sila.

"I'd like to read something to you. Please listen and try to remain open-minded and receptive. Can you do that?"

Sila felt like she was scowling but tried to look blank.

"There are people who would rather not interact much with others. These people have trouble expressing feelings and that makes it harder for them to join groups or form bonds with others. Many of these people have strong interests or attachments and can repeat things in a way that makes others not receptive to spending time with them."

She finished and looked at Sila, who asked, "Do you think that's me?"

"No."

"Oh. Okay."

Mrs. Holsing leaned forward. She seemed more at ease when she wasn't reading. "The term for this is *autism*. Have you heard of that?"

Sila nodded.

Mrs. Holsing turned back to the screen and read out

loud, "Lack of social connection heightens health risks as much as smoking fifteen cigarettes a day or having alcohol use disorder."

"I don't smoke cigarettes and I don't drink alcohol."

"Of course not. I'm sorry. I wasn't supposed to read that part. My bad."

Mrs. Holsing's cheeks were suddenly red and her nose made a few twitches. Her voice was softer when she turned back to Sila. She seemed embarrassed.

"Sweetheart, the question I'm asking is whether you would consider being paired with a student who has been diagnosed with autism. You don't have this condition, and yet you've become isolated. We think that might make a good pairing for the study."

"So you're asking me to volunteer for something?"

Mrs. Holsing brightened. "Yes. You were picked and I'm here to recruit you. There are all kinds of selection criteria. I don't think we need to really dive into that. This program is being done by the university. We sent out an explanation in the mail and asked all of our parents to sign consent forms, even though they are only picking a few kids. Your father signed."

Sila was growing more confused by the moment. "I'm not sure why you picked me."

"Well, to start, you're both bilingual."

Sila was shocked. "The other person speaks Turkish?"

"Spanish."

"Oh. Okay, but I don't know what you're asking me to do."

"You will be excused twenty minutes early from class. And you and your assigned partner will meet in the library."

"For one day?"

"For the rest of the school year."

"For three weeks?!" Sila was surprised at her own volume.

"Sila, please lower your voice."

"Sorry. Who do I have to sit with for twenty minutes a day?"

"Mateo Lopez."

10.

Sila had known Mateo for years.

He lived only six blocks away from her on the other side of Lincoln Avenue where there were houses, not apartments, lining the street. Trees grew in the strip between the sidewalk and curb and there was no overnight parking without a city permit, making the neighborhood at night look organized and secure. This was what people called "the fancy part of Cleary."

When Sila was in first grade she had to complete a sentence for back-to-school night. The printed form said:

My NAME is _____ and when I grow up MY GOAL is to_____.

Underneath the pronouncement each kid was supposed to draw a picture. The teacher helped her students complete the sentence and then they were all given a booklet with their answers, which Sila had kept. Her page said:

"My NAME is Sila Tekin and when I grow up MY GOAL is to live with a lot of animals and make the world better."

The picture she drew was of a cat, but it had a thick tail like a beaver.

Mateo had written on his page:

"My NAME is Mateo Lopez and when I grow up MY GOAL is to ride a lot of trains and also travel to Mars. But not on a train because there aren't tracks in space, which is very disappointing." The picture he drew was of a train, and there were dozens and dozens of lines going in all directions from it. Sila decided those were the tracks. Some of the lines went up into the sky and touched what looked like the moon.

So he was different from the start.

But knowing Mateo Lopez for years didn't mean she talked to him, because this boy was the quietest kid in the whole school. Of course he could speak. He just mostly didn't. There had been a time back when they were both younger when *all* he did was talk. At least that's the way Sila remembered it. Mateo would find something interesting and he would go on and on and on about it. But somewhere around third grade, as she thought back on it, he was moved to the last row of desks and he stopped participating. He turned in all of his assignments and usually got the best grade in the class, but he never raised his hand and the teacher no longer called on him. It was like a switch had been flipped.

As time passed Sila forgot that he once said more than anyone in her school. The kids got used to the new Mateo. Sila remembered being told by the teacher on a day when he wasn't at school that he had a "hidden challenge." The kids were all sitting on the sharing rug, which was where they went for something called "the respect circle."

After that day, Sila realized, the other kids didn't accept Mateo for being different as much as ignore him. She was guilty of that as well, which felt messed up now that she thought about it. He didn't look dangerous, but according to whatever report was on the computer screen in Mrs. Holsing's office, being super quiet could be as bad as smoking cigarettes and drinking vodka. And Mateo had been quiet for years now. A lot of diseases, she knew, were silent killers. He didn't have friends at school. That much she knew. But then again, she'd given hers up as well. She took some comfort in reminding herself that at one time she did have other kids in her life.

Twenty minutes before the end of the school day Mrs. Holsing's face appeared in one of the glass squares of the classroom door. Mateo, who she had been careful to not even once look at for the rest of day, noticed the woman just after she did. Sila put her books into her backpack, got up from her chair, and left the room.

Mateo did the same.

The other kids stared. A few people whispered. Sila heard the teacher tell them to return to their studies.

Sila and Mateo walked in silence behind Mrs. Holsing to the library, where they were shown to a small room that was used for meetings. One of the walls was glass and Sila made sure to get the seat where she could look out. Mateo sat opposite her in the chair with no view.

Neither of them spoke. After a few minutes a man came in. He introduced himself as "the Facilitator" in charge of the "Pairing." He told them he was going to be leaving, but that he hoped they would take this time to "get to know each other without the pressure of a formal classroom."

Sila and Mateo stayed quiet.

The Facilitator left.

That was a big relief.

On the table there was a stack of puzzles. There were playing cards. A chess set. Checkers. Two sketch pads with two sets of markers and two packages of modeling clay. They stared at the stuff but neither of them touched it, although Sila thought the markers and the clay looked interesting.

After an awkward amount of time they both took out books from their backpacks. Sila was reading a novel called *The Sweetest Sorrow*. She caught a glimpse of what Mateo had in his hands and managed to see the title *The Trouble with Gravity*. It was an adult book with the subtitle *Solving the Mystery Beneath Our Feet*. Sila just wanted to solve the mystery as to the point of being in the room with Mateo Lopez.

After what felt like four hours, but according to the clock on the wall was only twenty minutes, the Facilitator came back into the room and said they could go home.

Sila and Mateo stood up, got their backpacks, stuffed their books inside, and walked out the door.

Even though they were going to the same street and they had just experienced the same strange time alone in the library, they didn't exchange a single word, and didn't make any attempt to walk home together.

Sila let herself into the apartment and went straight to her room. She opened the curtain and looked out the window just as a train passed by. She sat there lost in her thoughts for a long time, watching the wind make the trees sway when she suddenly saw a boy walking a large dog on the path near the train tracks.

She knew that boy.

It was Mateo Lopez.

Sila closed the curtain, which was how her mother liked the room.

Had he walked there before and she'd never noticed?

11.

Hours earlier Gio had driven Chester Briot to Oregon First Bank on 7th Street because the ringleader insisted on cash for the purchase of his elephant. But the branch didn't have $41,000 in currency; they were able to give him only $10,000. Phone calls were made, and Gio and Chester went to four more bank branches in town to collect the rest.

It felt to Chester as if they were robbers, and at every stop he was getting more and more excited. By mid-afternoon the money had been collected, and two of the enormous Briot Family Circus trucks and one of the vans drove through the large wooden gates and rolled to a stop in front of Gio's pink farmhouse.

Veda was in the larger truck.

And a bear named Mr. Pickles was in the smaller one.

Gio didn't pay for the bear. Chester realized that someone like Giovanni Gardino only comes around once in a lifetime, and so he threw in Mr. Pickles as part of the deal, along with his metal cage, which had been custom built with steel bars,

rotating wheels, and a double-locked sliding door. Chester was turning over (besides the elephant and the bear) eleven fifty-pound bags of elephant supplemental feeding pellets, six bags of assorted rotting fruit, forty pounds of cull carrots (the ones that are twisted or crooked and not up to super-market standards), and five bales of hay.

There were also two metal eating troughs; an aluminum water tub; many lengths of ropes, chain, and rubber padding; a decorative pink harness with a matching custom-made saddle; three different ornamental headpieces with giant ostrich feather plumes, sequins, and gold braiding; six blankets; ankle bells made to fit around all four of Veda's feet; shovels and cans for poop collection; a special ladder and long-handled brushes for elephant bathing, as well as a box of tools to cut elephant nails and take care of Veda's foot pads.

The final item was an official, government-issued notebook with the title *Standards and Practices for Elephant Management and Care*. It had never been opened and was covered in plastic. Chester turned his back to Gio so that he could rip off the wrapping and bend a few pages to make it seem used. He stuffed inside a bill of sale from when he bought Veda years ago.

Not much came with the bear.

The truth was that Chester wasn't generous. He just didn't know who would buy his elephant supplies, and getting rid of the stuff meant he would be in a position to immediately unload both of the heavy-duty trucks and the supply van. He tried to sell the vehicles to Gio, explaining that they had been modified specifically for animal transport and he couldn't imagine how Gio would ever move Veda without it. But Gio passed. Veda was never leaving him to go anywhere, he said. Not if he could help it. And the bear wasn't getting much thought at this point.

Rodrigo, the person responsible for the elephant, lowered the custom liftgate on the truck and pushed up the heavy sliding door. He used the bullhook, which was the metal tool outlawed now in most states, to move the elephant backward. It looked like a long, metal spear, and in addition to the pointed end, there was a blade-like hook coming out of one side. It was the hook that did the talking.

Veda rested her back foot onto Gio's property and felt the clay-like soil, not asphalt or cement, beneath her. She didn't detect the familiar smell of portable toilets, overflowing commercial dumpsters, or the grease of deep fryers. She didn't hear cars. Or trucks. Or motors of any kind. There were no sounds of people. Or their loud music.

This wasn't a truck stop, a county fairground, a cheap motel, or a civic center parking lot.

Veda slowly lifted her trunk and let it sway gently in the afternoon air. The elephant inhaled the sharp, tingling smell of the pine needles from grand fir trees. She detected vine maple. White alder. The pungent smooth madrone tree bark. She got a whiff of the delicate pink manzanita blossoms. There was wild ginger growing somewhere. Cedar. Sweet woodruff. Western lark. Osoberry. Engelmann spruce. Sword ferns. Golden currant.

The elephant's body seemed to grow taller as her nose absorbed the variety and complexity of natural odors. Veda's enormous ears suddenly flared wide. She heard the wind rustle in the treetops and the sound of chirping sparrows, towhees, and buntings. Two bullfrogs called out from a ditch nearby, and somewhere close dozens of bumblebees buzzed in and out of a hive.

Veda heard it all.

It was a symphony to her.

It was the call of the wild.

The elephant moved away from her mobile prison and looked out past the farmhouse where she saw only open space. There was a sloping landscape of leafy trees, meadows, and in the distance, golden hills.

And then her eyes fell on Gio.

He stood perfectly still.

Veda turned to him. He didn't seem afraid. He seemed to be in awe.

The elephant took several steps forward and stopped. Gio stretched out his hand, and Veda's trunk extended to meet it. Gio whispered, "This is all yours now. This is your forever home."

Chester made certain the bear was moved in his wheeled cage out of the second truck and into the old barn so fast that Gio never saw it happen. The old man stood motionless alongside Veda, whose trunk was carefully investigating the top of his gray-haired head, strand by strand. Chester tried not to explode from sheer excitement. He had pulled off the highway to get donuts and would be getting back on the roadway only hours later with over forty thousand dollars in cash and without a two-ton elephant and a cranky bear. Chester had heard Gio's story as they collected money and had decided he was the one, not Gio, who was winning the state's Powerball lottery!

Chester's plan before he went into the Hole in One bakery (if he could say he'd even had a plan) was to try to find a zoo for his elephant. But Chester had never received an exotic animal permit. He didn't do the regular (and required by law) veterinarian checkups. He had never been caught breaking the rules because the circus was forever on the move, always wheeling into a new town, in a new state, with new officials. So as long as Chester kept printing out false documents and acting with great confidence and authority, he'd never had a problem.

But he had to get this deal done as quickly as possible before the enormous burden of elephant ownership sunk in and Gio had second thoughts. He needed to be somewhere untraceable before this eccentric old man wearing expensive bedroom slippers could change his mind. Or at the very least before the guy got his foot smashed when Veda went in the wrong direction.

Chester tried hard to look sad, but he wasn't sure it was very convincing, when he announced, as if into a microphone, "Veda, it is here that we say our goodbyes. This is where I leave you."

The elephant was having none of it. Veda's final act in the farewell charade was to drop her trunk to the ground, scoop up dirt, rocks, and pine needles, and in one well-aimed motion fling it all right at Chester.

He could have lost an eye.

Veda had scored a direct hit. After Chester recovered, wiping his cheeks with his sweater sleeve, he managed to sputter, "I'll miss you too. Don't be angry. Believe me, this is all for the best."

Pretending that the elephant had reacted harshly because she was so sad to see him go, Chester went straight to the large transport truck, slamming the door shut with such force that the whole vehicle swayed.

Gio watched Veda allow Rodrigo, her daily caretaker, to touch her hind leg, but as the man said goodbye, she wouldn't look at him. Rodrigo moved to hand Gio the bull-hook, saying, "Here. Use this to control her."

Gio shook his head. "You can keep that."

"You're going to need it. Trust me."

"No, thanks."

"She's stubborn," Rodrigo insisted. "You don't have to poke her hard. Just give her a nudge with this when you need her to move. She knows. Makes her afraid."

"I don't want her to be afraid."

"She's dangerous. Do you understand? She can kill you if she wants to—it wouldn't be hard. There are all kinds of ways for her to do that. Not just trample you to death."

Gio found the man's harsh tone unsettling. "You should go."

Rodrigo shook his head in dismay. He tossed the metal hook on the ground at Veda's feet and got into the truck. His last words before he started the engine were, "She's smarter than you think. And a whole lot stronger. Don't say I didn't warn you."

The man who had been dealing with the bear was already waiting in his truck with the motor running. He leaned out the window and shouted at Gio, "For a reward of a chunk of raw salmon you can get Mr. Pickles to ride a tricycle, especially if you got a whip in your hand. He can clap his paws together if someone sings 'If You're Happy and You Know It.' He can blow a few notes on a trumpet. I'm not saying he wants to do any of that. I'm just saying he can. But I'd leave him alone for a while. He's a real grump this time of day."

And with that, the three Briot Family Circus vehicles headed off the property and disappeared down the road. Gio wasn't sure it was possible, but he thought he heard

Veda sigh with relief once the high wooden gates closed behind them. He knew *he* did.

Chester Briot's euphoria over selling Veda didn't last very long. The ringmaster had no way of knowing that once Veda was gone from his daily world, he would be gripped with a sadness that was unshakable, unrelenting, and unsolvable.

A dark cloud hit the man and he was troubled by recurring nightmares where he was trapped in a cage, transported in a truck for miles on end, never to arrive at a destination. It wasn't just the persistent terrors that came to haunt him. From the day he sold Veda, Chester was plagued with dryness in his eyes that caused him to have problems blinking. It took a specialist in Salt Lake City to finally make the correct diagnosis: Chester Briot had keratoconjunctivitis sicca, or severe dry eye syndrome. His tear ducts were closing off. He could no longer cry. Going forward, every hour on the hour when Chester was awake, he needed to put artificial tears in his eyes.

Once the elephant was gone from his world, it was as if a curse had set hold. Chester didn't believe in such things, but if he could later trace back his various health problems (and he tried many, many times), it would all lead to the afternoon he sold Veda. Maybe it was something in the dirt the elephant had thrown at his face. Regardless, Chester would find himself thinking about her every day for the rest of his life.

Veda, on the other hand, would never think about him again.

12.

The first thing Gio did once he was alone with Veda was go inside his farmhouse to change out of his bedroom slippers. If the elephant moved in the wrong direction and he got in the way, she could easily break his arthritic toes. Or worse.

"I'll be right back. Just wait here," he had told her. He had put a full bag of red apples at her feet. They were, Rodrigo had said, a special treat.

It was only moments later, as Gio was tying the laces on his boots, that he heard a crash. He ran out of his farmhouse to find the apples still in a mound, but Veda standing with her right foot on the now-destroyed first step going up to the porch. She'd been trying to follow him inside.

"Are you okay?" Gio shouted. He wasn't worried about losing a wooden step or even an entire front porch. "I'm so sorry! I shouldn't have left you alone."

His only concern was for Veda. And she must have felt

that: She hadn't taken her eyes off of him. Gio reached for an apple and held it out. Veda's trunk carefully took it from his flattened palm.

She was such an amazing combination of power and grace, he thought.

Chester had explained that Veda was on the small side for an Asian elephant, weighing just over five thousand pounds. Yet from that moment on, she followed Gio around like the world's largest new puppy.

After he'd looked through the big pile of supplies that the circus people had dumped in front of the farmhouse, Gio remembered the bear. There had been so much excitement, he hadn't given any thought to his other acquisition. Mr. Pickles was inside his cage in the barn, moving around with agitation.

Veda, who had followed Gio, had been able to move right through the opening of the double doors, which were just tall enough to accommodate the top of her head. She stood at a distance from the bear cage, eyeing Mr. Pickles with what looked like little enthusiasm.

Gio found four enormous bags of cheap dog food piled in the corner of the barn. A case of grape jelly was leaning against the dry dog food. A note read:

MR. PICKLES EATS IN THE MORNING AND AT NIGHT. TEN CUPS OF DRY DOG FOOD EACH TIME. YOU CAN GIVE HIM ANY BRAND OF FOOD. IT DON'T MATTER. THE BEAR LIKES IT IF YOU PUT SCRAMBLED EGGS OR JELLY (GRAPE IS BEST) ON TOP. IT'S UP TO YOU. HE WILL EAT THE DOG FOOD WITHOUT THAT WHEN HE GETS HUNGRY ENOUGH.

HE KNOWS THE WORD "NO." SO SAY THE WORD "NO," AND BE VERY LOUD ABOUT IT.

MR. PICKLES HAD HIS CLAWS REMOVED WHEN HE WAS YOUNG. HE ALSO HAD FOUR TEETH PULLED. THE BIGGEST ONES. HE WOULD NEVER SURVIVE IN THE WILD BUT YOU STILL GOTTA WEAR THICK LONG-SLEEVE SHIRTS AND BEST TO PUT GLOVES ON WHENEVER YOU ARE NEAR HIM.

<u>DO NOT TURN YOUR BACK ON THIS BEAR.</u>
<u>EVER.</u>

MR. PICKLES LIKES TREATS. BUT HE CAN GET MEAN ABOUT WANTING THEM.

REMEMBER! YOU ARE IN CHARGE, NOT MR. PICKLES. <u>DO NOT ROUGHHOUSE OR WRESTLE WITH MR. PICKLES. EVER.</u>

HE HAD HIS INCISORS PULLED BUT HE CAN
STILL BITE HARD.

Gio put down the note. It was then that he saw an electric cattle prod leaning against the wall. There was a second note taped to the four-foot weapon. He was horrified as he took hold of the prod and read:

HE KNOWS WHAT THIS MEANS. IF YOU WAVE
IT AND SHOUT ORDERS HE WILL LISTEN. IF HE
DOESN'T, GIVE HIM A ZAP.
TWO ZAPS REALLY GETS HIS ATTENTION.

Mr. Pickles froze when Gio picked up the weapon. He watched like a statue as Gio carried the prod to a storage cupboard, tossed it inside, and shut the door. Gio then walked over to the metal enclosure to look at the bear more closely. He saw that the fur was mostly gone on the animal's elbows and parts of his legs. On his backside, his entire coat was flattened down to a smooth, greasy-looking carpet. Gio figured this could only mean that Mr. Pickles had been forced into the same position in his cage for far too long.

The thought of so much confinement combined with the electric prod broke Gio's heart. He immediately unlocked the cage door and unhooked the two security latches that held it firmly in place. He then slid the heavy metal panel open and stepped back quickly, all the while keeping his eyes on the bear.

At first, Mr. Pickles didn't move. Then the tip of his nose twitched. The bear stared at the open cage door.

At Gio.

At the elephant.

At the big, empty barn.

The look on Mr. Pickles's face seemed to say: "Is this some kind of trick?"

Gio was riveted as the six-hundred-pound mammal lumbered in slow motion out of the cage. He appeared a lot stronger once his whole body could be seen. The bear was thick, his step was heavy, and as he moved, the air filled with a sharp smell. Then suddenly his slow-motion hesitation came to an abrupt end and he switched gears. The bear was instantly a blur of speed as he went straight for the bags of dry dog food. Mr. Pickles ripped open the top sack in what to Gio was terrifying quickness. The orange, red, and yellow pellets of Feeling Free tumbled (with no irony, Gio thought) onto the dirt floor of the barn. But Mr. Pickles didn't eat a single chunk of the newly liberated dog food mess. He spun around, maybe expecting someone from the circus to appear from the shadows and start yelling (or worse).

When that didn't happen, the bear looked confused, and then invigorated! He returned to explosive action. Veda swung her trunk as if to say "stay away," and Mr. Pickles kept his distance. He was fast as he circled the barn, peering into the empty stalls, taking a roll in dirt clods, and then returning to his four feet. In a flash of moving fur he changed course and went straight past Veda and out the barn's double doors.

Gio couldn't believe that his own legs could still run hard as he took off after the bear. It was the first time in over twenty years that he'd been in a full sprint. Mr. Pickles went straight for Gio's farmhouse. His paws might have looked large and inept, but that was far from the truth. He bounded over the step that Veda had crushed and turned the knob on the front door as if he'd lived there all his life.

13.

Gio did his best to sound in control as he shouted a thunderous "NO!" But Mr. Pickles gave no indication that he'd ever heard the word before. Once inside the house the bear knocked over a coatrack, upended a lamp, and broke a big porcelain bowl on a side table. He went straight for the kitchen to the refrigerator, where he opened the freezer, and in only seconds was holding a gallon of chocolate mint ice cream in his front paws. He pulled off the top of the container and scooped the contents into his mouth in greedy gulps of pure pleasure.

Veda, standing outside at the kitchen window, watched as Gio ran shouting into the room. Mr. Pickles tossed the empty ice cream tub in Gio's direction and got hold of two frozen, single-serving chicken potpies. He ripped into the cardboard boxes, and his teeth snapped down hard. He seemed to have no trouble swallowing icy chunks of pastry and chicken with rock-hard gravy.

The bear next went for the non-freezer section of the

refrigerator. He got hold of two sticks of butter, swallowing them with the waxed paper still on. He tossed mustard, ketchup, and relish bottles aside, but when he came across a container of maple syrup he grunted so hard with obvious glee that snot came out of his nose. He tore the top off with his teeth, splattering cold, sticky sweetness onto the kitchen walls.

As Gio shouted "No" while waving a frying pan and then a mop, Mr. Pickles found a jar of pickles. He dropped the glass container to the kitchen floor, where it smashed. He then picked out six large pickles from the broken shards and ate them in a frenzy as Gio exclaimed, "Mr. Pickles really does eat pickles!"

The bear was a destruction derby. The mop and the frying pan were clearly doing nothing to stop him, so Gio ran to the hall closet. He pushed aside a wooden yardstick and a folding stepladder to grab a broom, then he hurried back into the kitchen waving the sweeper overhead just as Mr. Pickles downed eight eggs (whole in the shell). All Gio could do was swing the broom and shout "NO! NO! NO!!!"

Mr. Pickles gave zero indication that he cared about the broom. Or the elderly man shouting. The bear stuck his entire head back into the refrigerator. He had no use for a bag of pre-washed lettuce, a container of cranberry juice, or a bunch of celery. But with growls of happiness he ate a package of salami and a brick of cheddar cheese. Gio could see Veda outside the kitchen window, consuming apples as if they were popcorn kernels. It was as if he and the bear were some kind of television show.

Gio fired a can of Lysol and tossed boxes of Kleenex in an attempt to force Mr. Pickles out of the kitchen.

Nothing worked.

The bear continued to eat or break anything that came into his line of sight. But luck finally swung in Gio's direction when the animal picked up a portable radio. His paw hit the on button, which was set to the local classical music station. An opera was playing. The sound of a female singer hitting a high note sent Mr. Pickles running from the room and out the front door. Gio shouted after him, "So you like pickles, but you don't like sopranos?!"

The sun was going down as Gio surveyed the mess. It was catastrophic. He had no idea how to begin the cleanup, but that thought left his mind when he realized he had a large bear loose on his property and an elephant staring at him through the kitchen window.

When Gio came out onto the front porch, Mr. Pickles was

nowhere to be seen. It was truly shocking how fast the bear could run. Veda turned her body to the right and swung her trunk. Was she trying to tell him something? Was she indicating the direction in which the scoundrel had gone?

Veda followed behind Gio as he wandered around for an hour in the fading light, looking for the bear. Finally, admitting defeat, he returned to the barn. His only comfort was the thought that the stone wall was too high for Mr. Pickles to get over. At least he hoped that was the case. Gio put an old blanket in the bear cage and left the metal door open. Then despite being exhausted, he turned his attention back to his elephant. Gio took a hose and topped off one of the metal tubs with cold water. He then used a wheelbarrow to move one of the bales of hay into the barn. Lowering himself down into a folding chair, he watched as Veda ate the straw.

And ate.

And ate.

Veda finished what he would later find out was almost one hundred pounds of hay. Gio gathered together all the cushions from his outdoor furniture and carried them up a ladder to the barn's loft area. He got a pillow, two blankets, and a flashlight from the house, and settled in with a great view of the enormous animal below. He didn't want to leave her alone. He figured if Veda woke up and started wandering, he could at least follow her.

Once the food and most of the water was gone, Veda stopped moving. Her eyes fluttered shut and her breathing slowed down. And from high above, Gio understood that she had fallen asleep. The stillness of an animal that size, on her feet, filling her lungs in a slow, deep way, made Gio start to cry. He realized he hadn't wept since Lillian died. But now tears streamed down his face. He couldn't wait for Sila to see her. Even with all that had happened on this day—the longest day he remembered in his whole life—Gio knew he'd made the right decision when he bought Veda.

Because he knew at that moment that he already loved her.

It was after midnight when Gio, who hadn't eaten anything since the two donuts that morning so many hours before, climbed down the loft ladder and went into his wrecked kitchen. He stepped around the enormous mess and found a jar of peanut butter in a cupboard that Mr. Pickles had somehow missed. The bear also hadn't opened the bread box that Gio kept in the oven, where there was half a loaf of wheat bread. He got a knife and plate, and took his supplies back to the barn. He was grateful for the jars of grape jelly that the circus people had left. Gio headed back up the ladder to the loft and made three peanut butter and jelly sandwiches.

They tasted as great as any meal he'd ever eaten.

He had just started to doze off when he heard something down below. He turned on his flashlight to see Mr. Pickles. The bear was moving like he'd just attended the world's wildest New Year's Eve party. He had twigs and leaves in his fur, and mud caked on his paws. He did a slow turn to stare up at the harsh glare shining down from the loft.

Maybe he thought it was a spotlight, because he rose up on his hind legs and did a twirl that was surprisingly graceful. He clapped his paws together twice and then returned to all fours. Did the bear suddenly believe he was back performing in the circus? Or, having been born in captivity, was this his way of showing gratitude for the bounty of the day?

After a few rolls on the hard ground, the bear headed to his old cage. He reached in and pulled out the blanket that Gio had left, and then curled up next to the metal siding, wrapping a big part of his body in Lillian's mother's Depression-era cotton quilt. The bear was fast asleep in what felt to Gio like only a few seconds.

He snored loudly.

14.

Veda had nothing to say to the bear. And the bear had nothing to say to her. They were never friends. Just because they were both locked up in metal boxes didn't make that so.

He was a bear.

She was an elephant.

Veda had heard him come into the barn and was now half awake, her thoughts flowing in an uncontrollable way. She was exhausted and afraid. Would the sun appear in the morning, and would she find herself back inside the metal box, moving on the road to nowhere?

She stared through her dark eyelashes to the dirt floor of the barn. The past flooded all of her senses: She was born to a family of four. But five elephants were too many elephants. She was still drinking her mother's warm milk when she was loaded into the moving box and taken away.

She had learned to step up. And to step down. She learned to turn to the left. And to the right. She could lift

her trunk high. And then higher. And she could hold it. She could lower to her front knees and let a man climb up her face and onto her back. She could make her ears go wide. She could put all her weight on her back feet and rise up until it felt like she was crushing her own spine. She could steady herself in this position of agony as white-hot pain shot through her entire body. But she would do it. She had no choice. They had a hook. And they had the electric shock stinger. They used them.

The circus people could teach her to do many things. But they could not teach her to trust them. Or to ever forget her past. It had been twenty-one years. Veda shut her eyes and saw her mother. This happened every night. When you miss someone that deeply, the feeling can last for your own forever.

15.

Mr. Pickles was always in the moment. All day. Every day. He could stare at the hot ball of bright light in the sky until he could see nothing else. He could gaze at the moon and feel no distance. He could listen to the buzzing of a bee and hear the fluttering wings.

But his nose was what drove him.

The smells of the world were his language of love. He lived for every inhalation that entered his hot nostrils on the way to his enormous lungs. He could sniff a scent from miles and miles away. The smell could be sweet. Or rotting. He knew the odor of decay. The pungent pollen of a blooming flower. He understood mold. Fungus. The stink of the end. But he also knew birth. Renewal. The fragrance of a single tree blossom.

Mr. Pickles could smell the rain before the first drop hit. He could make out a single blade of grass pushing up through distant wet soil. He could grasp the savory. The unsavory. He lived for the smoke of meat curling skyward from an unseen

barbeque. The sweet tingle of caramelized sugar from cookies baking in a far-off oven was a game-changer. He smelled popcorn as it was poured fresh into a bowl, and a torn candy wrapper tossed into an open trash can.

And he wanted it all.

Was it any wonder he felt half out of his mind locked in a cage? Because Mr. Pickles's world was channeled through his nose, the slightest change of air direction brought new horizons. He had no past. He saw no future. There was only the now. The smell of this world. He was in it.

He *was* it.

And being set free from a traveling circus was heaven on earth.

16.

Lying in bed staring up at the ceiling, Sila thought about the day, almost a year ago, when her world changed. Everything that had happened since then was her fault. That's why she had trouble sleeping. And that's why she wanted to be alone at school. She had brought all of this onto her family the last time she wore the horribly unlucky shirt.

Her mother had come home early from work that long-ago Friday and sunk into the sofa, saying, "I was too tired to go to the bank to deposit my paycheck."

"I can't wait until I'm old enough to have a real job," Sila said, plopping down next to her mother.

She saw an envelope sticking out of Oya's purse, and since she liked looking at her mom's paychecks she pulled it out.

"Mom, this says Miguel Mendoza."

Before her mother could stop her, Sila had her fingers in the unsealed envelope and Miguel's check in her hand.

"Sila, don't do that," Oya said. "It doesn't belong to us!"

"I'm not spending it, I'm just looking. Hey, he gets more money than you."

Sila passed the check to her mother, who stared at the stub where the details of the payment were shown. Oya looked confused.

"He worked the exact same hours as me. But he got paid more."

"Does he do the same job?"

"He's a janitor. I'm a housekeeper. So yes. He cleans. Just like me."

"Has he been there longer than you?"

"No. He only started last year."

"So why does he get paid more?"

Oya didn't answer for a long time, but when she did her voice was hard.

"I think because he's a man."

That was the beginning of the end. Oya went to the Grand Hotel the following Monday and returned Miguel's check to accounting. Then she spoke to the general manager, where she made her case that the women in housekeeping did the same work as the men in janitorial and she wanted to know why the men were paid more. The general manager said he'd look into it, and the next Friday, Oya was told that the hotel was cutting back on staff. She was let go that day, even though she'd been Employee of the Month only two months earlier.

Minutes later, holding the coffee mug she kept in the workers lounge, she was waiting in shock in the parking lot for Alp to come get her. A woman approached looking for the service entrance. She told Oya she was interviewing for a position in the housekeeping department.

So the hotel clearly wasn't cutting back on staff. Oya had been fired for questioning the system that saw a janitor as different from a housekeeper. The janitors pushed vacuums and brooms. There was nothing they did that the women didn't do.

What happened was bad and then it got worse. The following month a certified letter arrived in the mail saying Oya's immigration paperwork was under review. A summons ordered Oya to immigration court. Her right to be in the country was being challenged based on a "tip" that her documents were incomplete. Further investigation revealed that Oya needed to return to the country where she was born and get new signatures on new documents.

It seemed simple when she left, but while she was overseas the rules changed for entrance to the United States. Oya Tekin was stuck. She was now waiting abroad, uncertain when she'd be able to come back to her husband and daughter.

Sila turned on the light and opened her bedroom door. It was so quiet. Living in an apartment building meant that there were always sounds. Other people flushing toilets in rooms above and below. Doors opening and closing. Strains of a television show played too loud or music from someone's unit. And the street had its own set of noises. And then of course there was the scheduled sound of the trains.

But right now everything had closed down. The world Sila knew seemed to be entirely asleep. Standing in the hallway she could see that her father had left a light on and the small living room was awash in purple shadows. Sila headed silently to a cabinet there and opened the bottom drawer. Inside was a shoebox tied with a ribbon. She removed the box and returned to her room.

Sila lifted the cardboard lid. She knew what was inside: all of her report cards. It didn't take long before Sila had what she was looking for. She unfolded the two pages and stared down. There were letters written in boxes, mostly G's and E's, which stood for *good* and *excellent*. But those notations didn't interest her. She flipped the second page over and read:

Sila is a wonderful addition to the classroom. She shows great promise.—Lillian Gardino.

There it was. Her signature. Her handwriting. She was gone now, but she had once been in Sila's world.

Mrs. Gardino.

Gio's wife.

The next morning, after waking up late and staring out the window at a few passing trains, Sila thought about pretending to be sick. The last thing she wanted to do was go to school. She came out of her room, still in pajamas, doing her best to cough and look sweaty.

"I don't feel well."

Alp motioned for her to come over, and he put his hand to her forehead.

"You don't have a fever."

"My stomach doesn't feel right."

"Eat some toast. And get dressed. You don't want to be late for school." He went back to reading.

Sila coughed some more but it sounded forced. Her father might fix cars for a living, but he could have been a doctor. It was hard to fake an illness with him.

She'd have to go to school, and she'd have to spend twenty minutes in the library with Mateo Lopez. It was hard to think of anything that was more awkward.

17.

Gio woke up in the barn loft and looked down to see a gray cargo van and a mound of brown leaves. He put on his eyeglasses and realized he was looking at a motionless elephant and a snoring bear. Like winning the lottery, this felt like a crazy dream, and he was deep into it.

He climbed down the ladder and tiptoed back to the house. With bright sunlight flooding through the windows of the kitchen, Mr. Pickles's mess looked even bigger. Gio could never allow Mr. Pickles to spend his life in a cage. He would never use an electric prod to get the bear to stay away from the farmhouse. He wished that he could just drive up to the state park in the mountains and let the big brown bear go free. But Mr. Pickles didn't have claws or any training to find food. He didn't understand he should stay clear of people.

Gio needed to find a home for the bear that his conscience could live with. He had no idea what he would have done without the Internet, because soon he'd located

a woman only three hours away who made rescued bears her life. Kimmie Bouttier already had seven bears, but Gio offered to pay for ten years of Mr. Pickles's food in advance, and Kimmie agreed to come get the bear.

Just after lunch she arrived with two workers and a big truck. Kimmie clearly had a way with bears. She was fearless as she approached, a thick wedge of raw salmon extended in her gloved hand. Mr. Pickles seemed to take an instant liking to the woman. And to her fish fillet.

In a matter of minutes Mr. Pickles was in his cage and heading for the Bouttier Bear Sanctuary. Gio stood on the road in front of the high stone wall long after they'd gone. He wouldn't miss the bear. He just wanted to be certain they weren't coming back.

Later that day Kimmie Bouttier sent Gio a photo of Mr. Pickles in his new habitat. He was (as could be predicted) eating. Behind him were seven other bears. Gio had read that most bears are solitary in the wild, but he knew they did form friendships and even alliances when in close proximity.

"Mr. Pickles," Kimmie Bouttier wrote in her email, "is destined to be the leader of the pack."

This made Gio feel that he'd done the right thing.

Once the big bear was gone Gio could focus his attention entirely on Veda. A change happens when someone takes on the responsibility for an animal. And this was on the biggest scale of disruption. All the elephant wanted to do was follow Gio around the property. But her meandering was also her way of eating and drinking, which Gio came to realize was a description of a free elephant's life. Elephants consume at least a whole bathtub's worth of water every day. And they need a huge amount of food. Veda right away started eating bushes and tree branches. Soon she went after entire trees.

Elephants are a lot like goats, Gio decided. They can and will eat almost anything. Veda pushed over a birch tree and chewed up the leaves, twigs, bark, and branches until finally even the tree's trunk made it into her stomach. Gio was at first shocked, then amused, and finally concerned. The elephant was some kind of bulldozer. He had to find a way for her to get enough food without eating everything in her path.

Veda took care of the water herself. While Gio was in the house making calls to arrange for a secure way to close the barn, she went down to the lowest area on Gio's land, which is where the big oak trees tower. A bed of thick grass and weeds grew there year-round. When Gio arrived, half out of his mind after looking for Veda for over an hour, he found her standing in a pool of water. She had eaten everything and dug her own drinking hole.

Gio didn't know there was an underground spring on this part of the property. But his elephant knew. She had ways of sensing things, he realized, that he could neither see nor hear nor smell. That afternoon Gio hired a backhoe driver to use his heavy equipment to dig ten feet down in the pebbly soil. As he made the area bigger it continued to fill up with water. By the end of the following day Gio sat on the rise of the hill and gazed down at the elephant, who was moving in a very large muddy pond. He knew it would always be his favorite part of his land.

That night in the barn loft, when Gio finally took out his phone, he saw a message from Alp Tekin. The replacement parts for his old truck had arrived. The two men made an appointment for Saturday, and Gio told Alp to tell Sila there was "a big surprise waiting for her when she came out to the property."

Gio hung up the phone and couldn't stop smiling.

18.

"I think he got himself a dog," Sila said as she and her father turned off the main road onto the gravel lane.

"That's as good a guess as anything."

"I hope a rescue that needed a good home."

When they drove around a bend she saw Gio sitting in his old truck, which was parked outside the gates. That was strange. Sila found herself wondering if everything was okay. As soon as they got close, Alp put down the window and Gio called out, "I was thinking it would be best if you worked out here today. Instead of inside on the property. I was lucky the truck started up."

He didn't offer more of an explanation, but he added, "And Sila, once we go behind the wall, no wandering around. We all stay together."

Sila shot her father a look. Exactly what was going on?

Alp asked what she didn't. "So you got yourself a dog? Is that it?"

Gio shook his head. "Nope. No dog."

Alp didn't stop there. "But you're worried that something's going to escape. That's why you want me to fix your truck out here?"

"Not escape, exactly. But yes, get loose, I suppose. I need to keep the gates closed."

Gio turned his attention to Sila. "Let's go in and have a look."

Sila stayed silent. Spending time with Mateo was giving her even more insight into the power of not talking. Her dad didn't seem very enthusiastic but managed a "Sure thing."

Once behind the wall, Sila could see that Gio was different. He was excitedly waving his arms in the air, saying, "I'm having a second gate put in here. Thirty feet forward. With higher fencing. That will give me a double entrance. It's being built right now."

Sila saw that concrete had been poured and thick steel poles were in place. "You're going to need that? A second whole entrance?" Alp asked.

Gio answered a firm, "Yup. For certain."

But he wasn't revealing more. Sila found herself getting irritated. Whatever they were about to see was making the old guy act nutty. Next he pointed to a new golf cart that was parked next to the farmhouse. "I got the cart yesterday.

That's one thing about money. You can call up and people will deliver! We're going to all take a ride."

"So is that the surprise? You got a golf cart?" Sila was interested but had been hoping for the dog.

"Nope. That's not it."

"I've always wanted to drive a golf cart," Sila said. But her father replied, "You're riding, not driving."

Gio whispered in her direction, "Maybe later you can give it a try."

Sila climbed on the back and sat in the rear-facing seat. Alp got up front. Gio slid in behind the wheel. They were barely seated before he had turned the key and the cart lurched forward. "Hold on. There's no seat belts in this thing."

Sila could see that he was pretty excited about whatever it was he had to show them. They passed tall trees, then an open space with yellowy, three-foot-high grass as they bumped along the dirt road that cut through Gio's property. This man owned a lot of land, Sila thought, and it was varied: rolling hills, open areas, and clumps of towering pines.

They'd been riding for almost five minutes when they started up an incline. Just before they were at the top, Gio slowed down. He timed it perfectly, because when they rolled to a stop the cart was right at the crest of the hill.

Sila looked down and saw a large, muddy pond.

With an elephant standing in the center!

And not just any elephant, but the magical creature from the donut shop. Sila gasped. Her father's mouth opened in shock. It was so unexpected.

"IT'S VEDA!" Sila shouted.

"You thought you'd never see her again," Gio answered.

Sila was dumbstruck as she watched one of the largest land animals in the world raise her trunk, swish her tail, and then stomp her front foot, making a big splash.

Sila was out of her seat in a crouch, her head hitting the cart's metal cover. She was in awe. "I can't believe it. I just can't believe it."

She wanted to get out of the cart and go down to the edge of the pond, but Gio wouldn't allow that. "Elephants are dangerous. And I'm still getting to know this one," he told her.

As they watched Veda move through the muddy pond, showering herself with blasts of water from her trunk, Gio explained how he'd bought the elephant on his birthday.

It was the first time in more than nine months that Sila didn't think about her family's problems. Her eyes stayed on the elephant as Veda dug up roots with her feet, ate tree branches, and at one point lowered herself down and rolled in the muddy shore. She was so large and yet so deliberate in her movements. She was powerful, but graceful.

Eventually, Alp said he should probably get to work on the truck, so Gio drove them all back to the farmhouse. After some assurance that Gio would stay up on the hill at a distance, Alp agreed that Sila could return in the cart with Gio to keep watching Veda.

It was there, sitting on the hill, that Sila turned to Gio and asked, "She's really yours? You're going to keep her?"

"She's here to stay. We're in this together now."

"I'm so glad she's not in the circus anymore."

"Me too. The owner was a strange man."

"Yes. But Mr. Gio, does anyone really own another living thing? I think you can only own stuff like sleeping bags and microwaves. The other things are just what you're supposed to take care of."

"Sila, you are so right. And as it turns out, I'm an elephant person."

"Me too."

It felt as if ten minutes had passed, not over an hour, when her father called Gio on his cell phone to say that the repair work on the truck was done. Sila's heart sank. When would she see Veda again?

Standing at the gate with her father and Gio, Sila said, "This is the greatest place in the world." She decided there was no harm in asking a question that had been burning inside her from the moment she first saw the elephant that day. "When can I come back to see her again?"

"Anytime," Gio said, adding, "And you can bring a friend."

19.

S ila's mother had always knitted sweaters and scarfs and hats and even socks for her only daughter. And now that she was gone, she was knitting on overdrive. Every week a box arrived from Turkey with something handmade for Sila or her father.

Sila didn't want to hurt her mother's feelings, but she found everything Oya knitted itchy and uncomfortable. Her father must have felt the same way, because he stashed all of his stuff from her in the hall closet. That seemed wrong, but Sila didn't say anything.

Her week had started out badly when a boy named Jordan had laughed at her, saying, "Your sweater looks like a lumpy old carpet." The kid was mean but kind of right. Sila's mother copied the intricate pattern of Turkish rugs for her designs.

When Oya had still been at home, Sila would walk out the door many mornings wearing a hand-knitted sweater and in the winter even a handmade scarf. But she would jam

the stuff in her backpack once she got near school. She was used to doing things two ways: She spoke two languages, Turkish at home and English when she was out in the world. So there were two ways to go to school: one to make her mom happy, and one to feel comfortable. She could do both.

But now things were different. Sila woke up earlier than normal on Friday and opened the shade, hoping a train would go by. She went to her bureau and removed the most recent of her mother's scratchy sweaters. She slipped it over her head. It was May. Summer was just around the corner. The sweater was uncomfortable and far too hot to wear in spring weather. But Sila had made her decision.

The back of her neck was sweaty and her hair was wet at the top of her braid. It had been a hard day, and not just because she was making a point to the universe about the value of her mother, as seen in the heavy sweater. The week had dragged on. She'd missed turning in two assignments and didn't do very well on a history test because she'd read the wrong chapter. Sila was having trouble concentrating. Her mind was not there in the classroom; it was with her mother and an elephant.

And then there were the twenty-minute "connecting"

sessions. She and Mateo Lopez had still not said a single word to each other. She felt bad that she didn't make an attempt to talk to him, but she thought he looked as disinterested in the whole thing as she was. Today would mark over a week they'd been reading books for twenty minutes in that airless room. Sila could hear the other kids whispering when they left class early every afternoon. Before, she would have cared what they said about her. But now it made no difference.

When it was time to go that day, Sila gathered up her things and silently walked out the door. Mateo was right behind her. They got to the library and found the Facilitator waiting. He always left once they were settled. Sila wondered if he was watching with a hidden camera, or maybe listening on a speaker. But today the Facilitator looked at her with real concern.

"Is everything okay, Sila?"

"Uh-huh," Sila managed.

"You're flushed. You should take off your sweater. I think you're overheated."

Something inside Sila snapped and her eyes filled with tears. She whispered, "My mother made this sweater."

The Facilitator stepped back as if afraid that she might

suddenly start sobbing. But before he could say anything, a low voice spoke out, "The pattern of Sila's sweater shows the ethnic, cultural, and religious pluralism that comes from one of the oldest points of civilization. Her family is Turkish."

Sila turned to look at Mateo. He continued, "She has her reasons for wanting to wear the sweater."

The Facilitator stared at the boy. "Yes. Thank you, Mateo."

Sila adjusted her backpack. "Come on, Mateo. Let's go home."

Once they were off the school property walking home under the leafy walnut trees, Sila said, "Thank you."

Mateo responded with, "For what?"

"For the sweater stuff."

"If you wanted to take off your sweater, you'd have taken off your sweater."

Sila stopped walking.

Mateo kept going.

Sila put her backpack on the sidewalk and pulled the heavy sweater over her head, leaving her in a cotton T-shirt. She stuffed the sweater into her backpack and ran to catch up with Mateo.

"Wow. That's so much better. It was like being rolled up in a carpet all day."

The boy didn't say anything. Sila added, "You're a good person, Mateo."

Again, he didn't answer. He kept moving, his stride long and deliberate. Sila noticed he was careful to step in the center of each concrete sidewalk square. They walked for another eight blocks in silence. But it wasn't actual silence.

Cars whizzed by.

A plane could be heard overhead.

There were squirrels making their high-pitched chirps.

Every sound seemed amplified as Sila began to think about Mateo's world. Was he listening to those sounds or was he hearing just his own thoughts?

He seemed both more focused and more distracted than anyone she'd ever spent time with.

Two blocks before the corner of Lincoln and Cleary, Mateo stopped. They had reached his house but he wasn't heading toward the door. Sila was unsure what to say. Maybe nothing was best. Then Mateo said to her, "Gravity gives weight to objects. The moon's gravity is what causes Earth to have tides. Gravity is why the planets circle the sun. The spheres are pulled in and reap the benefits of the warmth."

Sila nodded but she was unsure why he had picked this moment to bring this up. Mateo squinted up at the sun and then looked at his brick house. A large dog appeared suddenly in the window and began barking with excitement. Mateo was focused on that now. He headed straight for the front door.

Sila called out, "See you on Monday, Mateo."

He didn't answer.

She watched as he took a key from his pants pocket and let himself into the house. Once Mateo was inside, the frantic barking stopped.

Sila stayed on the sidewalk waiting to see if the boy or the dog would pass by the window. But that didn't happen.

Did Mateo think people looked right through him?

She knew *she* didn't.

At least not anymore.

20.

It had been a busy week for Gio. He'd had a metal enclosure built inside the barn. He'd watched a video posted by the San Diego Zoo, which was one of the best in the world, and he'd copied their design, hiring the welders he'd worked with at Chinook Modular Housing. He paid them double their rate to work after their regular shifts ended.

For most of the day Veda was now free to roam wherever she wanted on his acreage. Gio figured that it was good for her to explore. She liked to spend time down at the pond, but so far she always came back up to the barn at sunset. After so many years living in a truck, she seemed happy to go inside every night and fall asleep standing in fresh hay in the new metal enclosure.

On Wednesday night Sila ate her scrambled eggs and toast while Alp read his book. It was their regular routine until Sila said, "Dad, do you think we could go see Mr. Gio this weekend?"

"I could call and find out."

"Thanks."

"Just as long as I don't have to work."

"Right," she said. "And one other thing . . ."

"Yes, Sila?"

"Mr. Gio said I could bring a friend."

Alp was really paying attention now. Sila's dad had spent a lot of time encouraging his daughter to see her friends but had gotten nowhere, and after months of it, he'd finally given up. He looked truly excited as he said, "Really? Do you want to do that? Bring Porter? Or Daisy? Or Nala?"

"No."

"So a new friend?"

"There's a person from school I want to bring—he's not really a friend."

Alp's voice was no longer quite as bouncy: "A boy?"

"Yeah. He's in my grade."

"You've known him a long time?"

Sila nodded. "But he doesn't really talk. So it's hard to know him."

Her father's face said he didn't understand.

"I mean he talks to me. But barely. And at school he

doesn't speak to anyone. He used to. Back when we were younger. He used to talk all the time and now I'm thinking maybe they told him to be quiet."

Alp was silent.

"I haven't asked him if he wants to go. He doesn't know anything about it. But I think he'd like Veda."

"Does this boy have a name?"

"Mateo Lopez. When you call Mr. Gio you should find out what we can bring. You never visit someone empty-handed."

This was something her mother always said.

Minutes later, Alp made the call.

Gio said to come out on Saturday and to bring a water-melon.

Sila wasn't sure why she wanted Mateo to go with her. When they were together for twenty minutes in the library they still didn't speak. They did walk home together now, always in silence, until yesterday when he said goodbye before heading to his front door. That felt like a big deal to Sila. She called out "Goodbye" in return, and even though he didn't turn around or acknowledge her, she knew he'd heard.

Sila believed she hadn't said goodbye to her mother in the right way when she left. They both thought they'd be seeing each other very soon. She wished she could do it all over again. Goodbyes were more important than they appeared to be.

Since her father had said it was okay, Sila's plan to invite Mateo out to Gio's had been taking shape. She would wait until they were walking home, and then explain about the lottery winner and his big piece of property behind a stone wall.

But the next afternoon, as soon as the Facilitator left and she'd taken her seat in the library room, she blurted it out. "Mateo, I'm going to see an elephant this weekend. Do you want to come with me?"

Mateo looked up from his book.

His lips stayed in their permanent school position, which meant sealed.

He stared at her.

He blinked a few times, and when he finally spoke he said only, "I'll ask my mom."

That was it.

He had no follow-up questions. He didn't ask where the

elephant was or why they would be going to see it. There was no mention of time or how they would get there. Just "I'll ask my mom."

Sila found herself getting angry. Did he hear her correctly? She said an elephant. She felt like shouting now. But she decided to assume that he *had* heard. He just didn't react to things the way most people did. Her anger dissolved as she realized he didn't feel the need in that moment to know more. And she shouldn't either.

He would ask his mother.

That was enough.

When the twenty minutes in the room were over, they gathered their things and started the walk home. Two could play at this game, she thought. If he was the Quiet King, she could be the Quiet Queen. It required focus to keep your mouth shut. Since the day her mother had gone, she had that ability. Not much distracted her because she had the *big* distraction now. It was the thing that had changed the color of every room. But after she met Veda, the crush of missing her mother could be lifted by thinking of the elephant. So that's what she did as they walked, until they had reached his house. Mateo stopped at the walkway and without even looking at her said, "My mom works from home on Thursdays. You can ask her about taking me to see the elephant."

Sila exhaled with a kind of relief that made her shoulders lower as Mateo took a key and let himself into the house. Sila followed behind. She was uncertain what to expect, but when she saw brightly painted walls with bookshelves everywhere, she liked the place right away. And then from around the corner the dog came running. He went right into Mateo's outstretched arms and Mateo spoke to him in Spanish:

"¿Cómo te va, Waffles? Qué tal tu día?"

The dog spun in circles of pure happiness and then burrowed in between the boy's legs. Mateo got down in a squat and let the dog lick his face as he continued, this time in English, "Were you a good boy? Did you watch for squirrels? Did you sleep under my bed?"

Sila didn't move a muscle.

The Mateo she saw with the dog was not the same person she knew from school. It felt to Sila like the dog had some kind of magical power over him. Suddenly a voice called out: "Cariño, ¿eres tú?"

Mateo didn't answer.

The dog turned toward the voice, and then back to Mateo, and for the first time the animal seemed to realize that Sila was in the room. Waffles started to bark, sounding an alarm that a stranger was present. The voice again called to him: "Mateo?"

And moments later, his mom appeared.

21.

The teacup in her hand fell to the floor.

That's how startled the woman was to see Sila standing in the entryway. She rushed right back out of the room saying, "Goodness! Let me get paper towels!"

Sila crouched down to pick up the porcelain pieces of the broken cup. Mateo kept playing with Waffles.

His mother came back with a roll of paper towels and a sponge. She and Sila buzzed around like two bees gathering the shards and mopping up the splattered tea. Mateo and his dog stayed at a distance. With her hands full of what was once the teacup, Sila followed Mateo's mom through the dining room, where a computer was sitting on a dark wood table next to stacks of papers and a cell phone. They continued into the kitchen to put the pieces into the trash and then awkwardly both washed their sticky hands in the kitchen sink.

"The tea had honey," Mateo's mother explained.

Sila nodded. She felt awful. The broken teacup was her

fault. It looked like a fancy cup. Maybe it was a family heirloom.

"I'm really, really sorry."

"Oh, please, no. I wasn't expecting Mateo to have anyone with him. That took me by surprise. It was all my fault."

Sila wasn't buying that. But then she realized it was possible—no, it was highly probable that she was the first kid who had ever come home from school with Mateo.

"So you're a friend of my son's?"

Sila nodded. "I'm Sila Tekin."

"I've seen you before at school. I'm very happy you are here. I'm Rosa Lopez. Please call me Rosa."

"My parents like me to call adults Mr. or Mrs."

Mrs. Lopez nodded, and then asked, "Do you want an after-school snack? Or a glass of something to drink?"

Sila realized that what she wanted was to go home. But when she looked toward the door she saw Mateo, who had entered the room. He was so quiet when he moved. He would make a great detective. Sila cleared her throat. "No, thank you. I'm here because on the weekend I'm going with my dad to see a friend who has an elephant, and I wanted to know if Mateo could go with us."

Mrs. Lopez's whole face squeezed up in surprise. "An elephant? A real one?"

Sila was pleased that the woman at least had what she felt was the right reaction.

"Yes. A real elephant. My friend bought her from a circus. He lives outside of town on an old farm. But it's not really a farm. He just bought the place because he won the lottery and that's what he wanted to do with the money. His wife was Mrs. Gardino. From school."

"Mrs. Gardino? Who taught second grade?"

"Yes. Mateo was in my class."

"I remember her. Very well," his mother said.

Sila took a closer look at Rosa Lopez. She wore boxy eyeglasses and had short, thick, dark hair that was cut in what Sila considered to be a very stylish way. Sila wondered for a moment what she would look like if she cut *her* hair short.

Sila then continued, "She was my favorite teacher. But she died and now me and my dad are friends with her husband, but that was a coincidence."

"Goodness, I heard about that. A few years back."

"Over four years ago."

"Right."

"Anyway, her husband bought an elephant. I was there when he first met her. We'd be gone for a couple of hours. On Saturday."

Sila looked over at Mateo. His gaze was on a bookcase, where she could see an entire row of books about trains. He suddenly crouched down and put his face into the side of the big dog. Sila didn't know if that meant something. His mother said, "¿Quieres hacer eso?" Mateo didn't answer.

"I don't see why Mateo couldn't go," she said to Sila. "It's not dangerous, right? Is it dangerous? The elephant is in an enclosure or something?"

Sila decided it was best not to answer the question about the enclosure. "No, it's not dangerous. My dad is all about safety."

Mateo's mother seemed a strange combination of very excited and very confused. She stared at Sila, who suddenly just wanted to leave again. Being around a mom, even one who wasn't hers, was really starting to get to her.

Sila moved through the dining area back toward the front door, saying, "Okay. Well, you can think about it."

She squeezed by Mateo and Waffles. She had left her backpack on the floor when the teacup fell. She picked it up in a one-armed scoop and got her other hand on the front doorknob. She had her back to Mateo and his mother when she said, "It was nice to meet you, Mrs. Lopez."

In seconds Sila was on the sidewalk heading down Cleary Road.

She almost didn't look over her shoulder because she felt certain no one would be watching.

But she was wrong. Mateo and Waffles were both at the window.

22.

Mateo went up to his room after Sila left and took out his homework. It was always the first thing he did after school, because he wasn't allowed to play video games until his mother could see he'd done everything that was due the next day.

But on this afternoon when he looked at the assignments, he found he had trouble concentrating on the work because he was going to see an elephant on Saturday. And with Sila, who until recently had never seemed to him to be interesting in any way.

Elephants, he knew, were amazing animals and this trip was going to be something very different from a regular weekend.

Mateo put the schoolwork aside and went online to begin reading about elephants. He was intrigued to learn that at one time elephants had been transported on trains, which endlessly fascinated him. He found a picture of an elephant getting off a Ringling Brothers Circus train in 1963 and there

were little kids sitting on a curb very close by, which seemed dangerous. Mateo studied the picture, taking in every detail. He then found pictures of elephants in Africa, with people on safari. He was interested in the details of their camouflage clothing.

Then he started thinking about Saturday. Why did Sila ask him to go with her? Could he trust her to be nice to him? What if it was some kind of trap? The kids at school had teased him in the past and he had learned to keep his guard up. Thinking about Saturday was now making him anxious.

He had been at his desk for more than two hours when his mother knocked on the door, announcing it was dinnertime. He looked at her and saw that there were stains on the bottoms of her pant legs. That must have happened when she dropped the teacup.

Mateo hated it when he broke something. His mother was not expecting to see Sila, which was maybe why she dropped the cup. Or it was possible that she didn't have a good grip on the handle and the accident was just bad muscle control.

Or it could have been both things, because sometimes there was a main factor and a contributing factor as well. The world was more complicated than people thought.

23.

By Saturday morning Sila had experienced a change of heart.

Rosa Lopez had called the night before to say that her son would be ready on Saturday for the trip. Why had Sila asked Mateo to go see Veda? What was she thinking? Would he bring his backpack filled with books and disappear into one? Would he say or do something to irritate Gio or her father? She was going to be responsible for him, and while he was in some ways the most predictable person she knew, he was also capable of unusual behavior.

It was too late to pull the plug on the plan. Maybe, just maybe, he would change his mind at the last minute. Sila closed her eyes and imagined her father's car pulling up to the brick house and Mrs. Lopez coming out the front door to deliver the bad news, which would actually be good news.

"*Mateo woke up with a sore throat. He can't go with you today. Don't bother asking him again to see an elephant because he doesn't like large animals and he gets carsick and also the color gray annoys him. But anyway, thanks for think-ing of him, Sila."*

Mrs. Lopez would then hand Sila something wrapped, which would turn out to be a dish of homemade chocolate cookies with nuts, saying *"You can keep the plate. We don't need it returned. It belonged to the set with the broken teacup. I never liked the stuff, so I'm getting rid of all of it."*

Instead, two hours later, Sila and her father drove down Cleary Road, and from a block away she could see Mateo standing as straight as a Popsicle stick at the edge of the curb. He wasn't wearing his regular uniform of jeans and a blue shirt. He had on camouflage pants, a camouflage jacket, and a camouflage hat with flaps.

Why was he dressed like a soldier?

Sila felt embarrassed for him. But then she realized there weren't other kids around to make fun of his clothing. And from what she'd seen, a person couldn't easily upset Mateo even if they wanted to. He went through life his own way and apparently today that meant looking like the character in the old cartoon who battled Bugs Bunny. He was a modern-day Elmer Fudd.

When Alp pulled the car toward the curb, Mateo didn't move a muscle. Alp gave Sila a look. She whispered, "I told you he was . . ." She searched for the right word. She didn't want to say "strange." That felt mean. So she said, ". . . different."

Alp put the car in park and Sila got out. As soon as she did, the front door of the house opened and Mrs. Lopez emerged holding a grocery bag. She must have been waiting inside at the window. Alp turned off the engine and opened his door to introduce himself to the boy and his mother.

"I'm Alp Tekin."

"Rosa Lopez. Nice to meet you. This is my son, Mateo."

Alp turned toward the boy. "Hey, Mateo."

Mateo was focused on getting into the car. He didn't say hello. He opened the car door and climbed into the back seat. Sila winced. Did he hear her father?

Sila could see that Mateo's mother seemed very nervous. She shifted the grocery bag in her arms and managed what felt to Sila like a forced smile.

"Thanks for doing this."

Alp replied, "We're looking forward to it."

Mateo never caused trouble at school. Ever. So was Mrs. Lopez worried because they were going to see an elephant? Maybe she was afraid of animals. Lots of people are.

Rosa Lopez's gaze went from Mateo back to Sila and Alp,

and then she came out with: "Hey, I was thinking . . . I could come along if that would make the trip easier."

Alp didn't seem interested in that idea and had started back around to the driver's side of the car as he answered. "Sila says she has your cell phone number. We can check in with you. Would that make you feel better?"

"Yes. That would be great," she answered. She then extended the grocery bag toward Sila. "I packed tuna fish sandwiches for you guys. And there are chips and almonds in here too. Plus cookies and a thermos of lemonade."

Sila wondered if the cookies were chocolate. She couldn't stop herself from asking, "What kind of cookies?"

"Peanut butter."

Sila hoped her disappointment wasn't too obvious.

Mrs. Lopez added, "Mateo eats a lot of peanut butter. And a lot of tuna fish."

"Both good things," was Alp's response.

Mateo's mother lowered her voice. "My son has a tuna fish sandwich every day for lunch. He's not very adventurous when it comes to food. It's easier if I stay in his lane."

Moments later Sila and her dad were on their way with Mateo, four large watermelons each weighing over twenty pounds, and the grocery bag with the sandwiches, chips, almonds, cookies, and lemonade.

Mateo stared out the window in the back seat.

Sila sat up front.

Alp kept his eyes on the road.

Sila again questioned why she'd bothered to ask Mateo to go, but there was no turning back now. He was sitting behind her rhythmically tapping her seat with his left foot. It could have been annoying, but Sila decided to feel it as the beat of music no one in the car but him could hear.

Alp rang the bell at the entrance to Gio's property, and this time they had to drive through two sets of gates. The newly installed second pair was made of metal and gave the place even more of a fortress quality. Sila hoped Mateo might comment on how unusual it all was, but he didn't say a word.

Gio was waiting on the porch. He seemed different to Sila, and it took her several moments before she realized why.

"You cut off your beard!" she exclaimed after rolling down her window.

"I did."

"You look younger."

"You think so?"

"It's a good look. I like it."

Alp parked the car and the kids got out. Sila found herself wishing Mateo had worn his jeans and T-shirt, but she realized that was her problem, not his.

"Mr. Gio, this is my friend Mateo."

"It's just Gio."

Gio extended his hand, and Mateo hesitated, but then to Sila's relief he stepped forward and shook it. He then looked away into the distance as if someone was calling him.

Sila leaned close to Gio and whispered, "He might be nervous about being here."

Gio whispered back, "We'll try to make him feel at home."

"We brought four watermelons, and Mateo's mom made us all lunch. My parents always say that when you go visit friends you should ring the doorbell with your elbow."

Gio looked confused, so Sila explained. "Because your hands are full—with the gifts you're bringing."

24.

t felt awkward, but they all climbed into the golf cart. Gio and Alp sat up front and Sila and Mateo got in the back. Everyone but Gio held a watermelon, and the fourth melon rested underneath Sila's feet.

The golf cart moved more slowly with four people and four watermelons on board. The tires seemed to sink into the road, and twice the cart bottomed out, rubbing the ground. Alp offered to get out and walk, but Gio insisted he stay put. Sila didn't mind traveling at this sluggish speed because it gave her time to see things she hadn't noticed before. Towering pine trees grew in clusters, and the enormous boulders they passed were flecked with color from moss and lichen. Sila wanted to ask Mateo if he agreed that even the rocks were cool-looking, but whenever the road got bumpy he shut his eyes. Sila wondered if he was getting carsick. Or in this case, golf-cart-sick.

A hawk flew overhead and a handful of sparrows

buzzed at all angles, working to keep the bird of prey away. Sila saw a bald eagle perched on the limb of an oak tree. Mateo opened his eyes, and Sila pointed up to the spectacle. The bird wasn't bald. It had a head of soft-looking white feathers and a beak and legs that were bright yellow. The eagle called out what sounded like a long, shrill whistle with a chirp added in. Sila wished she could make the same noise.

The entire time they were in the golf cart driving through Gio's property, Mateo gripped the edge of the bench seat. Sila thought he seemed miserable, but everything changed when they arrived at the summit of the hill and looked down to the pond.

Veda was waiting with anticipation. Sila figured that even though the cart was electric and pretty quiet, the elephant had probably heard them approach.

She called out gleefully, "Hey, Veda!" The elephant made her happy in ways she couldn't explain.

Mateo seemed different when animals were around. Sila watched as he let go of the side of the seat and his face took on a totally new expression. He was relaxed in a way that Sila had seen only when he'd been playing with his dog.

Sila asked for her father's phone and took pictures. They

were large and the elephant was small, but it was a real elephant—that much was clear in the photos. She texted the pictures to Mateo's mom and then returned the phone to her dad, asking, "Can we give Veda a watermelon?"

Sila was hoping Gio would take them to the edge of the pond, but instead he said, "Why don't you let them go from up here? They'll roll down the hill."

As much as Sila wanted to get closer to the enormous animal, the idea of watching watermelons spiral down the hill sounded great. She got out of the cart and Mateo wordlessly followed. Sila went first. She set her watermelon on the ground and let it go. The melon started rotating slowly, but as it continued downhill it gathered speed. It hit the pond with a splash, and she and Gio and her father cheered. Mateo's fingers spread wide and his hands flapped in a rhythmic way. It wasn't clapping. But it was a celebration.

The group watched from their high vantage point as Veda headed to the melon. She wrapped her trunk around the twenty-pound fruit as if it were a grape, lifted it out of the water, and popped it into her mouth. With a single jaw motion she crushed it in an explosion of pink juice and smashed rind.

Alp was impressed. "Whoa! There's no question Veda loves watermelon."

Sila agreed, adding, "She's so strong but also kind of delicate."

"In brute strength, there is no mammal stronger than an elephant," Gio said, adding, "Mateo, you're up."

It was Mateo's turn to send a watermelon down the hill, and now Veda was ready. Mateo was cautious as he set the watermelon on the ground. He let go, and this time as the spinning fruit came toward her Veda kept it from hitting the water by stopping it with her foot.

Sila cheered, "She's a soccer player!"

Sila took the melon that her father was holding and released it down the hill. This time the rotating watermelon hit a sharp rock at the wrong angle and it split apart, sending red chunks in multiple directions.

Mateo's first words that day loud enough for everyone to hear were: "We should have brought more watermelons."

Sila started to laugh and after a long moment Mateo started laughing too. It must have been infectious, because soon they were all laughing and Veda was stamping her feet in the pond, making the water splash. Sila decided it was her way of joining in too.

At exactly noon Mateo turned to Sila and said, "It's almost time for my tuna fish sandwich."

The tone of his voice made it clear that eating was a big priority. Gio put the golf cart in reverse as Sila said good-bye to Veda. She could have stayed all day watching her. The elephant changed how she felt about the world. It took away her anxiety about her mother. It made her optimistic about life again.

They arrived back at the farmhouse and got the food out of Alp's car. Then they all sat together at the old picnic table on the front porch. Sila didn't ever eat tuna fish sandwiches because she didn't like the idea of fish that came in a can, but there were small pieces of celery and bits of cut-up apples mixed in the tuna fish on a very interesting seedy bread, so it tasted pretty good. Her father and Gio both commented on the crunch of the thing.

Mateo ate his sandwich in silence, all the while staring out at the property. When he was done with the tuna he removed a small ziplock bag with seven almonds and carefully ate each one.

Gio did most of the talking, explaining to the group, "I'm refining how I feed Veda. I have hay and grain delivered, along with a wholesale order of carrots, onions, and sweet potatoes from a produce distributor. A truck comes every Monday. And I made a deal with the gardeners who work at the college. I pay them to bring all their clippings here. The grass, the branches, everything. It's a lot of green stuff."

Sila asked, "You can't just order elephant food?"

"Oh, I do that too. There's a place in Indiana that makes exotic animal supplements. The elephant pellets come in fifty-pound bags. I mix that in with fruit and grain. It's got all the vitamins and minerals she's supposed to have. Veda spends pretty much all day eating. Believe me, the only thing worse than a hungry elephant is being a person trying to *feed* a hungry elephant."

Sila was sympathetic. "It takes a lot of effort just for me and Dad to put together a meal."

"I've never worked harder. But I've never felt so good about it. I've got a five-thousand-pound reason to get up in the morning."

Sila noticed that Mateo had been staring at the results of all the elephant feeding. He seemed alarmed as he pointed to the bread-loaf-sized elephant turds that were all over the property, and said, "The poops should be gathered up."

Gio laughed. "She's a dung factory, that's for sure."

Mateo continued, "It needs to be organized. Put in one place. It's not good to have it everywhere."

Sila suddenly saw Mateo's point. "There are a lot of flies and who knows what else surrounding each of those poop piles."

"Well, maybe, Mateo, you're right," said Gio.

Once the sandwiches and chips and almonds and cookies were all gone, Mateo again asked about Veda's bricks of dung.

"Mateo and I could just pick up some of the stuff." Sila smiled at Gio and saw he was considering the situation.

"Okay then, I'll pay you."

"You don't have to do that. We want to do it. Right, Mateo?"

He was already on his feet. There were two wheelbarrows next to the barn and he was heading toward one.

25.

Alp had work gloves in his car and the kids each put on a pair. It was decided that they would take the manure to an area behind the barn. As Alp and Gio sipped lemonade at a distance, deep in conversation, the kids pushed wheelbarrows. When they had collected everything Veda had dropped around the farmhouse and in the barn, they started picking up dung on the dirt road that led toward the pond.

Time slipped away. Alp and Gio had been on the front porch talking for over an hour. Alp didn't get the chance to sit outdoors very often. He worked. He came home. He took care of his daughter. Then that cycle repeated itself. Since his wife had been gone, he hadn't wanted to leave Sila alone. They didn't go to the park or even take walks like they used to do. Alp missed that. He understood now that Sila probably did as well. Alp checked his watch and called out reluctantly to the kids that it was time to go.

Sila hollered back, "You've got to see what we did!"

The kids directed the two men behind the barn to an elephant turd pile.

"Well, will you look at that?" Gio said. "It's like a one-story mound of brown bread loaves!"

Alp shared only part of his enthusiasm. "Until you get close. The stuff has a pretty strong smell."

Gio laughed. "I've already gotten used to it, but I guess it's a good thing I don't have close neighbors."

The old man reached into his pants pocket and took out two twenty-dollar bills. "You kids did a great job," he said as he handed Sila and Mateo each the cash.

Alp made an attempt to stop him. "No. They were happy to help clean up."

Sila agreed. "My dad's right. We did it for fun."

Mateo added, "And because organizationally it was the correct thing to do."

But Gio held firm. "Nope. It was a job. I won't have it any other way. You get paid for work."

Gio's words echoed in Sila's ears: "You get paid for work." Suddenly she saw an opportunity for herself this summer. School would be out soon. In the past Sila had found jobs babysitting some of the little kids who lived in the apartment building. She'd also helped a woman down the street pull weeds in her garden. But this would be something a thousand times better. She could save the money and use it to help her mom. She would be outside. She would be with Veda. She would spend time with Mr. Gio Gardino. There was nothing that sounded better.

They were walking toward her father's car when she said rapidly, "Gio, the school year's almost over. Do you think I could come out here to work this summer? I could clean up after Veda, and put the hay in the barn. I'm sure there are all kinds of things that need to be done. Maybe Mateo could work with me out here."

Sila wasn't sure why she was including Mateo. He could be annoying. But at the same time, it didn't feel right to leave him out. He was standing there at her side listening to her make her case, and she wanted to be a caring person. What difference did it make if he only wanted tuna fish for lunch or if he kicked the back of her seat? He didn't ever judge what she did—at least she couldn't think of a time that he had. Gathering up the elephant turds had been *his* idea. How could she leave him out now?

Mateo didn't say anything, but Alp did. "Sila, listen, you can't just ask—"

Gio interrupted, looking right at Sila. "I was just thinking how great it would be to have you two kids out here to help me."

"You were?"

"You could be my first real employees. I've had other workers, but no one yet who comes every day."

Sila tried to keep her excitement in check. "Really?"

"Yes. Really."

"Mateo and I live on the same street. Once school's over, we'd be able to ride our bikes out here."

The boy at her side was staring at the leaves moving in a birch tree. The wind had suddenly picked up. Was Mateo paying attention? Sila's father certainly was. Alp's voice was agitated. "I don't know about riding your bike and I really don't know if it's safe for you kids to be out here with the elephant."

Gio responded, "I would never put the kids in danger."

Mateo looked up. "I would like to be put in danger," he said, adding, "Also, the elephant poop could be worth money. It's not every day people have access to something like that."

Sila wondered if this was true. Mateo was an expert in a number of things. Sila smiled at Gio and decided to make it seem like this was something she and Mateo had discussed. "We've got a whole plan about what we want to do with the stuff."

There was no plan. But Mateo didn't contradict her, which he could have done.

Sometimes, Sila decided, saying you have a plan is the first step in making one.

It was agreed that nothing was agreed, which is actually a form of an agreement as far as Sila was concerned.

After one more trip in the golf cart to the pond to see Veda, they said their goodbyes and found themselves back in the car heading home. Alp turned on the radio, which was set to the local classical music station. Sila was going to ask if they could listen to something else when she heard from the back seat, "Clementi: Symphony Number Two in D." Alp looked over at his daughter. Sila only shrugged. They kept the radio on the classical station for the rest of the ride.

As soon as they pulled up to the curb in front of Mateo's house, his mother came out the front door. Mrs. Lopez was halfway down the walkway when she called out anxiously, "How did you do? How was the day?"

Mateo strode toward the front door without answering.

His eyes were on Waffles. Sila could see the dog jumping up and down at one of the front windows. Mateo didn't say goodbye to Sila or her father, and he didn't say thank you for the time together. But he also didn't say hello to his mother as he passed. Sila got out of the car with the empty grocery bag and thermos in her hands.

"Thanks for lunch. The sandwiches were great and I don't even like tuna fish."

"So you had a good time?"

Alp turned off the engine and stepped out of the car. Sila liked that he was polite that way. "It was a lot of fun," he said. "And I think your son enjoyed himself."

"I'm just—I'm, well—I'm so grateful to you for taking him."

"Our pleasure. He's a good kid."

Sila had never heard Mateo described that way before. Mateo was interesting. He was smart. He was a really different kid. Sila looked at Mrs. Lopez and could see that she was about to explode with happiness, so she offered up, "I took a lot more pictures. They're on my dad's phone. I can send them to you."

"That would be fantastic! And I sent the first picture to my parents. And also to Mateo's father."

Sila didn't think whether or not it was polite before asking, "Where's his dad live?"

"In Dallas." Mrs. Lopez then volunteered, "He's an aerospace engineer. Consumed with his work, really. He doesn't see Mateo much."

So his parents didn't live together. But by choice. Sila felt bad about that.

Mateo came back outside with Waffles on a leash. It was just the opening Sila needed. "What's Mateo got planned for the summer?"

Mrs. Lopez looked from Mateo back to Sila as she said, "Well, my first idea was to send Mateo to see my parents in Mexico City."

Mateo gave the leash a single tug and Waffles sat down. He then said, "But I'm not doing that."

Mrs. Lopez continued, "So then we started looking into coding camp. There's a program at the university for kids with high mathematical aptitude."

Mateo shrugged. "I don't know if I'm going to that."

Sila looked at her father. She could tell he wanted to leave. But she pressed on. "Today an opportunity came up for Mateo and me for the summer."

"Opportunity?"

Alp answered before Sila could. "My daughter would like to help out at Mr. Gardino's property this summer. I'm not sure it's going to happen. It only came up today. There's no decision made on that."

Mrs. Lopez turned to her son. He said, "Yeah. Me and Sila could go out there together."

It felt to Sila as if she had been waiting for this cloudy Oregon moment. Mateo was standing beside her now, and the two of them had a kind of force she didn't believe she'd feel on her own as she said, "I know you work. And so does my dad. Mateo and I would be outside all day and get a lot of exercise because besides the work, we could ride our bikes there and back."

"Ride your bikes?"

Mrs. Lopez looked skeptical.

She took a few moments, then answered, "I don't know. I need to think about it."

Mateo leaned back down to pet his dog. "You always say I spend too much time playing video games. There's no computer involved in pushing a wheelbarrow. Only I bet at some point in the future robots will be able to do that."

Alp put his hand on Sila's shoulder gently. "We need to go now, honey."

Sila nodded and turned toward the car. As she opened the door she looked back at Mrs. Lopez and said, "You work from home on Thursdays, right?"

Mrs. Lopez nodded. "I do."

"We could talk about it more then. I could come over after school. What do you do again, Mrs. Lopez?"

"I'm a lawyer."

Sila's father spoke once they were back in the car. "I haven't said yes to any of this, Sila."

"But you haven't said no."

"I'd worry about you out there."

"I appreciate the caring part, but we can't worry about disaster all the time."

"I don't think I do that. Do you think I do that?"

Sila nodded. "Because of Mom."

Alp exhaled in a long, slow way. "I'm sorry, Sila."

She realized her father had just spent a big part of his day driving her and Mateo out to see an elephant. He could have tried to get an extra shift at work and earned more money. She wasn't showing her gratitude. She leaned over and rested her head on his shoulder.

"No, I'm sorry, Dad."

He didn't say anything, and Sila shut her eyes. When she next opened them, they were pulling into their parking space at the apartment building on Cleary Road.

26.

That night in her room Sila set to work making a drawing of Veda.

She could have looked at the photos she took on her dad's phone, but she decided to make the picture the way she saw Veda in her mind's eye. The end result found the elephant to be enormous and Gio's pond small. She may have gotten the proportions wrong, but she was expressing what she felt. At the bottom of the drawing she wrote her father a note:

> Papa,
>
> Thank you for today. I know I'm lucky because you and Mom are people who took risks in your lives. You did that by leaving one country and going to another one for a better life.
>
> If we hadn't both been out to meet Gio and to see Veda, I would have to explain to you that he is a good person, and that I feel something bigger than

words when I'm with his beautiful elephant. But you've been there, so you know.

I want to work at Gio's this summer.

I want to be with Veda.

I'm hoping you let me.

Love you, Sila

Veda was in the barn inside the newly built metal enclosure, which guaranteed she was secure for the night. Gio had put out fresh hay, refilled her water, and gone into the farmhouse. He had returned to sleeping in his bed under the comforter that Lillian had made another lifetime ago. He could sometimes imagine that his wife was there beside him, unseen in the darkness. There were times he put a pillow where her body should have been, tricking himself into believing things were different. His thoughts were of her now, but then shifted to Sila and her friend. They had both known his wife. She had been their teacher. Lillian's students filled the place in her heart that would have held her own children.

Did he feel so connected to the young girl because she'd known his wife? There was something about Sila that brightened his day. It was her spirit. She was like Veda. She confirmed to him that the world was still filled with surprise.

For the next few days Sila and her father didn't talk about her upcoming summer vacation or Veda or Mateo Lopez. But Alp taped Sila's note with the drawing of the elephant onto the refrigerator door. She took this to be a good sign.

On Wednesday, she spoke with her mother for almost an hour, staring at the computer screen as Oya talked about the weather and different relatives, and finally her mother sang to her as she did when Sila was little. Oya called the tune "The Sila Song." Sila felt like she couldn't swallow while she was listening.

She didn't say anything about her proposed plan for working at Gio's, and she didn't bring up Mateo. She had decided her mother had enough to worry about. That week Sila and Mateo had read their books but not talked in their twenty-minute sessions at the end of the school day. They had a real connection now, so there was no need to do more than pass the time in the stuffy room.

Did the Facilitator know they always walked home together? Did he see that they ate lunch at the same table? Did he realize Mateo had given Sila half of his tuna fish sandwich every day this week and that she had given him a package of almonds and a piece of pita bread? Were they passing or failing the experiment? It made no difference to them.

On Thursday as the two kids approached Mateo's house, Sila said, "I want to come in and see your mom. Is that okay?"

"Yeah."

Then Mateo's attention shifted. He would be seeing his dog. Mateo took out his house key and they went inside to a routine that looked joyous on both sides of the kid/dog equation. Mateo turned into a different person briefly. Waffles went crazy. While that was all happening, Rosa Lopez appeared, this time not holding a fragile teacup.

"Hey Mrs. Lopez."

"Sila . . . what a surprise!"

"Remember? I said I was coming over."

"Yes. You did. Forgive me. I wasn't sure if you really meant that."

Mateo and Waffles were on the floor wrestling. They were both making squealing sounds.

"Can I get you something to drink? It's hot out there today."

Sila would have liked tea, but that might remind Mateo's

mom about the broken cup, so she shook her head. "No, thank you."

Mrs. Lopez stared down at her son. Her eyes narrowed. Sila looked over. Did he have a rubber dog bone in his mouth? "Mateo!" Mrs. Lopez shouted. "What have I said about that?"

It was unclear if Mateo released the toy or if Waffles just gained an advantage during the distraction, but the dog took off into the living room.

It was too much work making small talk with an adult she didn't know, so Sila got right to the point. "Have you thought any more about what Mateo will do this summer?"

Mateo was still on the floor, but now he sat up.

Rosa Lopez looked uncomfortable. "The plan is for him to go to coding camp."

Mateo got to his feet as Sila continued with her appeal. "Not everything you need to learn in life happens when you're sitting at a desk. Having a good time causes you to be smarter. I'm not making that up; I read it somewhere online. It turns out the brain expands in a good way when a person is having fun."

Mateo looked over at his mother and said, "At school they told us we're supposed to keep a journal this summer.

I feel like I'd have more to write about riding my bike and helping an old guy with an elephant than going to coding camp."

His mom seemed surprised. "I haven't heard about the journal assignment."

Sila could feel something shifting. "They are saying it's to show we used our time wisely, whatever that means. But it's really so that we remember what we were like years later when we reread it. At least that's what I think. There hasn't been a lot about this school year I want to remember. I'm hoping the summer is different."

Mrs. Lopez and Mateo had no idea what she was talking about, but neither of them pressed for an explanation.

Sila had rehearsed the last part of her argument in her head a few times, so her delivery was solid. "What if we went out to Gio's and you got to meet Veda and, of course, Gio? You might see it differently after that."

27.

On Saturday Rosa and Mateo Lopez were at the Tekins' apartment building at ten in the morning. Sila came out carrying two gallons of apple juice. She was excited as she climbed in the back seat of their car. She looked up to the second floor and saw her father standing at the window. She waved and he waved back.

Mateo was up front with his mother and he wasn't wearing his camouflage outfit. Instead he had on new blue overalls with his regular green T-shirt and a red bandanna tied around his neck. A straw hat was on his head and he was holding leather gloves. He looked like a scarecrow, which was better in Sila's opinion than Elmer Fudd, the cartoon rabbit chaser.

Sila hoped she sounded cheerful as she said "Good morning." Mateo was silent but his mother answered, "Good morning!" Sila held up the containers. "I brought apple juice for Veda. I read online that elephants like flavored water and fruit juice."

"That was very sweet of you."

"Thanks."

"How will she drink it?" Mrs. Lopez asked.

"I'm not sure. Maybe we could put it in a pail and she could sip it through her trunk."

Mateo didn't look up, but he was obviously paying attention, because he said, "People think elephants drink that way, but they don't. Her trunk is really a nose and an upper lip. They can suck stuff into the trunk, but then they shoot it back out into their mouths. It's not a drinking straw."

At the exact same time, Sila and his mom both said, "I didn't know." Then they both laughed.

Mateo added, "It might be the most amazing body part in all of the animal kingdom."

Mrs. Lopez took her car out of park and into drive. "Okay then, let's go see one of these things."

They hadn't gone far before Mrs. Lopez said, "I hope I get to meet your mother soon."

Sila tried to keep her face expressionless. She wasn't sure it was working. She managed, "She's traveling right now."

"On business?"

Sila considered how to answer, but then decided to go with the truth. "No. She has immigration problems. She's not in the country."

"Oh no, really? I'm so sorry, Sila. How long has she been gone?"

"Two hundred and eighty-four days."

Mrs. Lopez gasped. "Ohmygosh, that's awful!"

Sila could hear Mateo exhale in a long, wheezing way, and she suddenly felt so much worse. Yes. It was awful. So awful, it wasn't something to be shared. Sila closed her eyes. She wasn't going to cry. Not now. Not here. Then she blurted out, "It's not her fault. She didn't do anything wrong."

Mrs. Lopez looked up into the rearview mirror. "Oh goodness, I'm so sorry. Of course not. I didn't mean to pry. I just . . ."

Sila still had her eyes pressed closed. Then she suddenly had another problem. Her stomach lurched as if she'd been punched. This was not good. She called out, "Could you pull over?"

Mrs. Lopez swerved somewhat recklessly to the side of the road and put on the brakes. Sila opened the car door just in time to vomit in the gutter.

Mateo's red bandanna saved the day. He untied the thing from his neck and wordlessly extended his hand to the back seat. Sila used the cotton cloth to wipe both her face and then the edge of the car door, which had caught part of the splash of her morning breakfast.

She sat back in her seat as Mrs. Lopez fumbled a string of "Are you okay?" mixed in with very sincere apologies. Sila finally managed to say she was all right and that they should get back on the road. She mumbled to Mateo, "Thanks for the bandanna."

She didn't expect him to answer her, but then she heard him say, "You can keep it."

No sooner were the words out of his mouth than Mateo started to laugh. Sila immediately started to laugh as well. Then Mrs. Lopez joined them, albeit with some nervous energy mixed in.

And then Sila realized that the best part of what was happening was she'd never heard Mateo laugh hard before.

Gio was happy to see the group. And equally as excited to learn Rosa had tuna fish sandwiches. Plus there were not just peanut butter cookies and chips this time, but a tin of caramel corn. After introductions were made and the sand-wiches were placed inside the farmhouse in the refrigerator, Gio got a bucket for Sila's two gallons of apple juice. Then they piled into the golf cart and went down to the pond.

Gio rolled to a stop at the crest of the hill. Veda wasn't in the water. She was standing at a distance from the pond in an area with five-foot-high manzanita bushes. Her trunk rose to inhale the odor of the visitors. She then backed up, positioning herself behind a birch tree while she watched them.

"She sees I've brought guests."

Sila whispered, "Is she trying to hide?"

"I think so. But she's an elephant, so that's not easy."

Maybe having decided the new people were worth investigating, Veda stepped out from behind the birch tree and sauntered into the open.

Gio called out, "Hello, Veda! We've got company!"

Rosa managed, "Oh my. She's so big!"

Veda's tail swayed from side to side like a dog's. She moved her head in a similar fashion. Then she turned back toward the birch tree.

Gio shook his head knowingly. "She's going to show off."

Veda approached the tall tree and put her forehead up

against the trunk. She then stepped forward, using her body weight in an assault on the birch tree. The tree wobbled and then roots began snapping, rising up from the pebbly soil at the elephant's feet. Veda pushed harder and the tree made a ripping sound and then popped up from the ground and fell over with a thunderous smash.

No one moved in the golf cart, but Sila whispered, "Holy cow." Then Gio said, "Holy elephant," adding, "She'll eat that tree now; pretty much every last scrap."

As if on cue, Veda began putting branches into her mouth, crunching bark and leaves.

Gio worried that this display of strength might be too much for Mateo's mother. But he was wrong. Rosa Lopez looked thrilled. She had turned her attention from Veda to her son, who, along with Sila, was transfixed.

Sila asked, "Mr. Gio, where was Veda born?"

"I don't know. I didn't find out. That day was just a blur. But Chester said her parents were also in a circus. They were all Asian elephants."

"So you think she was born in the U.S.?"

Gio was uncertain. "Yes. Probably."

"So she's an Asian American elephant."

Gio thought about this. "Good point."

"But do animals still belong to a part of the world if they've never been to the place?" Sila asked.

"I think it's just a way of talking about what kind of elephant she is."

"What about people?" Sila continued. "You could say I'm a Turkish American. My father and mother are Turkish. But I feel like just an American. With Turkish parents."

Gio answered with: "I'm sure there are certain things from your parents that other kids you know don't have."

Rosa joined the discussion. "I'm from Mexico. But I came here as a little girl. I speak Spanish at home to Mateo most of the time. The culture around you becomes so much of who you are."

"I'm not sure what culture even is," Sila said.

"You kids are lucky to have such interesting heritage," said Gio.

"I guess. But everyone has a heritage."

Mateo had been silent, and now he spoke. "Cultural heritage is the selected legacy of both physical and intangible attributes of a group passed from one generation to another."

Gio nodded. "Mateo, you have an impressive mind."

"Thank you."

Sila added, "I don't even totally understand what you just said, but Mateo, I agree."

28.

After they'd returned to the farmhouse and eaten the lunch that Mrs. Lopez had brought, Sila and Mateo got the wheelbarrows and started elephant poop collection. As they rounded the corner behind the barn they both abruptly stopped. Was the big pile moving? The mound they'd made just days before looked as if it was alive. As they stepped closer Sila realized it was covered with birds.

"Mateo, what's going on?"

Sila and Mateo saw larks, magpies, blue jays, and crows pecking at the pile. The birds at once all took flight, landing in nearby trees, watching the two kids with what felt like irritation. With the birds gone, insects could be seen circling in the air, forming a moving cloud of gnats, dragonflies, bees, and flies. The teeming crust of the poo pile had ladybugs, grasshoppers, and beetles mixing with moths, butterflies, and spiders.

Sila waved her arms like a windmill to scatter the flying swarm, and then crouched down to get a better view.

"Look at all the ants! And the larvae. It's infested with bugs!"

Mateo got a shovel and stuck it into the decaying dung, revealing dozens of reddish-gray worms. Sila stepped back. "It's like a horror movie!"

They both edged away, and the birds, impatient to return to their feast, dove down to the pile.

Sila turned to Mateo. "We made the world's greatest bird feeder!"

And for the second time that day she heard him laugh.

They went to get the adults. Gio hadn't been back behind the barn and he had no idea that Veda's manure was causing such an explosion.

"This is proof that changing one thing causes a ripple effect to everything else," he said. "In the last few nights I've seen a skunk, two possums, and a raccoon. So I think it's not just birds and bugs that have found a new home. Up until now I wasn't sure why."

Mateo pointed up at the utility wires. There was a line of thick-tailed gray squirrels staring down at them.

Sila bent close to the ground. "I think these are mouse turds."

"There's never just one mouse," Sila heard Mrs. Lopez half whisper.

Mateo stared skyward again, and Sila followed his gaze to a red-tailed hawk circling directly above. Gio noticed it too. "That's a beauty. I heard owls hooting last night. I'm guessing that's all part of this."

Sila was pleased. "Do you think your place is turning into an animal sanctuary?"

Gio laughed. "It's already an elephant sanctuary."

Mateo's mother wondered, "Have you seen any deer?"

Sila had an idea. "You should put up security cameras. You could see what's going on out here at night."

"I'm not sure I want to know."

Mateo looked down from the sky to the manure pile. "I do."

"It's not just animals." Mrs. Lopez ventured closer to the manure. "All kinds of plants are sprouting in here."

Sila crouched at Mateo's mother's side. "I see what you mean."

"Veda eats a lot of vegetables and grains with seeds," said Gio. "Maybe some of it just passes right through."

As they walked back to the farmhouse Gio found he was wishing even more than usual that Lillian could be there. She used to say the best way to teach something was to show it, not just tell someone about it. That gave him the resolve to put up cameras. He would position them inside and outside the barn. Maybe he'd even put one up by the pond. It was obvious to him that the elephant poop was a powerful thing that was altering the habitat of this part of the Willamette Valley.

They stayed later than Sila would have imagined. Driving home she stared out the window uncertain whether the trip was a success. She knew that it had been a great day for her and Mateo, but what was his mother thinking? What would the summer bring?

When they'd gone to say goodbye to Veda, Gio had walked down to the edge of the pond with her for the first time. She held the old man's hand as Veda waded toward them. Sila stood as still as stone, clutching Gio's hand tightly as the elephant's trunk took a sniff of the top of her head. They weren't just getting to know each other. They were learning to trust each other. That was the beginning of real friendship.

Sila knew that Veda woke up each morning to a better world. But she didn't know that the elephant watched the sun at the end of the day turn the green hills to gold. Or that Veda began to understand more than the patterns of her new existence. There was an ever-changing sky overhead. And the red earth at her feet. There was water in a large pond with always-muddy shores. There were shrubs and trees and grass and brambles, bugs and birds, and a constant, fluttering wind. But the most important things were the wise man making the decisions about her life and the young girl who came to visit.

At night when Veda drifted off to sleep she could not believe her good fortune. The endless road was over. She had been released from prison into a world filled with kindness. She could now remember the things from the past that brought her joy. In a daze before sleep she would see her mother. Veda felt her giving her strength.

Veda was the dreamer in this dream.

29.

Sila was in her room when her father called out, "Come look at this with me! It's from Gio."

At the mention of his name Sila bounced up off her bed and into the kitchen, where her father had his laptop open. They both watched footage of a mountain lion making an attempt to scale the stone barricade around Gio's property.

"Look at that!" Alp exclaimed.

"Wow. Dad, it's a cougar, right?"

"It is. And he didn't come from a circus. He came from the mountains."

"But not to see an elephant," Sila said. "I bet he wanted some of the furry animals at the poo pile."

"Gio's going to have to start getting rid of that stuff."

"That's why Mateo and I want to help."

"We'll see. I haven't said yes."

"But you haven't said no. And that's the start of the breaking-down-a-parent process."

As far as Sila's and Mateo's parents were concerned the first obstacle was figuring out whether it would be safe for the kids to ride their bikes to Gio's. The beginning of the trek would be on quiet streets with designated bike paths. That didn't appear to be dangerous or confusing to navigate. However, once they were heading out of town onto the old highway, the kids would have to cycle on the shoulder, where there were broken and rough sections, or worse, nothing but loose gravel.

It wasn't practical to follow the kids in a car for a test run, so Mrs. Lopez said she'd bike out to Gio's with Sila and Mateo. The truth of the matter was that the kids had no problem with the expedition, and the gravel areas on the old highway were their favorite part. The only one complaining once they arrived was Mateo's mom, who kept saying "My butt is killing me." Sila wasn't even very sweaty. Mateo's only issue was that he didn't think his bike helmet fit right. Sila admitted hers didn't feel right either. She thought Mateo knew what he was talking about when he said, "Maybe every bike helmet feels like it doesn't fit right."

Once they were on the property the kids went to work with Gio, cleaning up the barn, refilling the water troughs, and putting out hay. Mrs. Lopez helped for the first half hour, but then excused herself to go to the farmhouse porch and return phone calls for work.

Sila and Mateo decided to take a look at the poo pile. In only days it had undergone even more transformation, gaining new life. Yeasts, smuts, mildews, molds, and mushrooms had sprouted up. Wildflowers and snarls of blackberry were creeping up the dunghill. There were weeds and stinging nettles spreading in all directions, and fiddlehead ferns popping skyward.

If something wasn't done, Sila thought, the elephant wouldn't be the biggest concern on the property: The menagerie of life that her poop brought would be the bigger issue.

After they'd eaten lunch, they loaded into the golf cart and headed to the pond. Mateo and his mother stayed up on the hill as Gio walked Sila down to the water's edge to see Veda again. Gio had a bag of peaches. While they fed the fruit to the elephant, Sila sang a Turkish folksong. It was something her mother had always sung for her. Sila figured it was the peaches, not her singing, but Veda started to rock from side to side, swaying in a way that could only mean contentment.

Watching from a distance, Rosa no longer had a question as to how her son should spend his summer. This experience would be more valuable than coding camp. But maybe more important, she thought as she stole a glance at her son, this possibility had all come from him. She wasn't the guide.

Once Mrs. Lopez agreed that Mateo could ride his bike with Sila out to Gio's, her father had no choice but to give in as well. He and Sila decided to keep part of the summer plan from Oya. She knew about the elephant, and that they often went to visit Gio, but it was decided she didn't need to hear other details. She didn't need one more thing to worry about. Oya's next appointment at the embassy in Ankara would be in sixty days. And that felt like an eternity.

Sila sat in her room that night waiting for a train to pass. As she thought back on the day, she wondered why she hadn't paid much attention to Mateo before she'd been put in the program at school with him. Of course she knew him, but not the way she did now. She hadn't ever bothered to question why he didn't talk in class or why he spent time alone. She had to admit to herself that she hadn't ever cared. Now she had to ask herself why she hadn't made more of an effort. He was quiet, but he had a lot to say.

She wondered what were other things in her life that she ignored. Sila remembered reading that poor people gave a bigger percentage of their income to charity than wealthy people. Was that because people who didn't have the money to be comfortable filling basic needs understood what that felt like? Did it make them more generous? Did her own pain and sorrow over her mother's absence force her to be a bigger person? Were people more compassionate because of their own difficult experiences?

The school year ended with the Facilitator giving Sila and Mateo each a gift certificate to the bookstore on Willamette Street and a container of sugar-candied peanuts. Sila was excited about both things.

"I'm going to buy a bunch of books as soon as I can get my dad to take me over to the shop," Sila said as they walked home. "But I'll start the peanuts now." She popped open the can and ate a handful. "They're really good."

Mateo handed her his container. "Take mine. I don't like peanuts with sugar."

Sila was pleased. "Okay, thanks!"

The Facilitator had also given them each an envelope, addressed to their parents. Sila pulled hers out of her backpack. "Should we read the letters?"

"Didn't you say you were never again going to open anything not addressed to you?" Mateo asked.

"Did I say that?"

"Yeah."

"Oh. Well, I say a lot of things."

"That you don't mean?"

"I mean it when I say it, but I'm open to changing my mind," she answered.

Sila returned the letter to her backpack, but when she got to her apartment she decided to look inside the envelope. Her father wasn't yet home from work. Sila closed the door to her room anyway for privacy.

The letter read:

> Sila Tekin participated in a program to connect students who have been determined to fall outside the norm for communication and interaction skills. Sila is a very curious, very determined, very considerate girl.

We have evaluated her as independent, sensitive, and empathetic. We see a bright future for your daughter.

E. Pope, Director Children's Outreach

Sila folded the letter back up and returned it to the envelope. She couldn't decide if the letter made her feel good or bad, so she hid it under the kitchen sink near her unlucky shirt. She knew that if it hadn't been for "Connections," she wouldn't have come to know Mateo. But a new friend didn't bring back her mother or keep her father from sleeping most nights in the living room with the TV on. The letter said she had a bright future, but would they have told her parents if she *didn't*? *"We see a lot of trouble ahead for your kid."* Would they have written that?

School was officially done for the year.

On Monday they would start at Gio's.

That was her focus now.

30.

Mateo left the letter from the Facilitator on the kitchen table. The envelope was addressed to his mother, not to him. After spending time with Waffles he took the snack that had been left for him on the counter and went up to his room. But instead of playing a video game, Mateo sat down on his bed and closed his eyes. He wasn't a fan of bright light and yet he thought it was curious that when he was out at Gio's, it didn't bother him. He knew that when he was distracted the things that could make him uncomfortable were much easier to bear.

This school year had been different.

Sila was his friend.

Having a friend could be a scary thing, because a friend could turn on you. That had happened in the past.

He was worried about that now.

When he heard his mother come in the back door from the garage, Mateo looked at the clock and saw that almost two hours had passed. He knew every sound of her home-

coming. He recognized his mother's computer bag being set down and then Waffles's paws scurrying across the hardwood floor to greet her. There was the noise of the glass jar with the dog treats opening and closing, and the snap of Waffles's jaws as he gobbled down the bone-shaped goody.

Unlike Sila, he wasn't very curious about what had been written by the Facilitator. Sitting in the library all of those days, he had never been sure what to do. He had read his books and worked to not flap his hands or do something that might cause a disruption.

Isn't that what they wanted from him? To make things easier for the other kids?

Mateo had feelings and thoughts and ideas about everything. In the past he had found that they were often ignored or treated as meaningless by people who didn't understand how he expressed himself.

He was different from a lot of kids, and he hadn't changed in that room in the library.

But Sila's attitude toward him had.

31.

The bike ride wasn't the same without Mateo's mom trailing behind. In the beginning heading down Cleary Road together, Sila felt free. But once they were out on the shoulder of the old highway, the opposite thing happened and she was tense in a way that she didn't remember. Mateo followed behind her, so she couldn't see what he was up to. She worried that she might be going too slow or too fast at times.

She was relieved when they were off the highway and on the back road with almost no traffic. Once she could see the gates to Gio's, she turned to look at Mateo. He was pedaling standing up, and he called out as if they'd just won a major race, "We made it!" Maybe it had been stressful for him as well.

Gio was waiting for them out front. He too seemed relieved. "I'm so glad to see you two! How was the ride?"

Sila answered truthfully, "It was longer than I remember."

"Every day it will get shorter. Because you will come to know the route." Gio turned to Mateo. "How'd you do?"

"I need a new helmet."

Sila started to sigh with frustration, but then she realized she wasn't his mother. She needed to be patient with the world. That's what her father said when she complained about waiting for her mother. And she knew she would need patience to get to know Veda and not expect too much too quickly. Mateo didn't have the same reactions to things as most kids. The key to their friendship was to not expect him to.

Gio outlined the day. They would start by spending time at the pond with Veda. Then they would set about doing chores, which mostly consisted of cleaning up and organizing.

At the pond, Veda came right up to Sila.

"Good morning, Veda."

The elephant extended her trunk, and Gio handed Sila an apple from a large bag. Veda took it right from her hand. Sila spoke to her. "I missed you. And I thought about you a lot."

Veda's large black eyes stayed focused on her.

While Sila fed fruit to the elephant, Mateo took off to

walk around the pond. He said he had measured his own stride, which he had decided to round up an inch and a half to thirty-six inches, or one yard. He was going around the pond counting his steps in order to calculate the size of the body of water. He called out, "Assigning numbers to objects is what allows us to compare things."

Veda turned to watch the boy. The elephant absorbed what happened around her in an amazing way, Sila thought.

The sun was higher in the sky when they arrived back at the farmhouse. Gio went inside, and the kids headed to the barn to fetch work gloves and their wheelbarrows. Mateo looked up into the shadows and said, "What's that?"

Above their heads, obscured in darkness, a creature stared down with shiny eyes.

Sila whispered, "Is it a rat?"

"It's too big to be a rat."

Mateo pulled a small flashlight from his pocket. Sila wondered if he always carried it or if this was part of his preparation for Gio's. He pushed a button and a surprisingly powerful bluish light appeared. Mateo took a step closer to Sila and then aimed up at the rafter. The animal they now saw looked like a huge rodent wearing an enormous, shaggy fur jacket. But once the beam of light hit, a transformation occurred. The thick coat seemed to organize itself into a sphere of sharp wires.

Sila's mouth dropped open. "Is it a porcupine?"

"I think so."

"Is it just one, or are there more?"

Mateo moved the flashlight across the support beams as he said, "A family of porcupines is called a prickle."

"You're making that up."

"I don't make stuff up."

Sila didn't answer, because in the time she'd known Mateo, she did realize he was intense about getting his facts right. Sila stared at the animal overhead. "She's beautiful— in her own way."

"How do you know it's a 'she'?" Mateo asked.

"I don't. I'm just guessing. We better tell Gio."

The porcupine, like the weasel that Gio had found sleeping in the front seat of his old truck the day before, seemed to be part of the explosion that all started with the dung pile. The new wildlife made Gio very happy, but Veda's waste mound, and the animals that came to be part of it, were clearly getting to be a problem. On the bright side, the elephant poop was a great fertilizer. There had to be a use for that.

From that day forward, he had Sila and Mateo take the fresh elephant bricks to an area on the other side of the stone wall. They called this new area the Wasteland. It was Gio who started singing "I'm going to Wasteland, Wasteland, Memphis, Tennessee." After that, Mateo repeated the line over and over and over again. It was, they discovered, taken from a Paul Simon lyric that Gio said was one of his wife's favorite songs.

Gio made calls to local plant nurseries and explained that he had what he believed to be some kind of miracle growing material, and that is how the Wasteland became a business. A woman showed up the next day with a pickup truck, and the kids helped her load the bed of the vehicle with Veda's bricks. She gave them money before she drove off. At first they didn't feel comfortable taking it, but Gio told them that saying thank you was the right and first response to any act of business.

Sila and Mateo were put in charge of the fertilizer operation. They were helping with Veda's food and signing for deliveries, and they were riding with Gio in the golf cart. All three of them were learning about elephant care. But also about the outdoors. And when Sila was busy, working hard outside in the sun, she was able to push the loneliness of missing her mother aside. She was able to take deep breaths and exhale.

At the end of the first week as they got on their bikes to ride home Mateo said, "We are lucky to be here."

"You're so right," said Sila.

She started to pedal off, and then turned to look over her shoulder and said, "Do you want to lead the way back home?"

In seconds Mateo's bike zoomed right past her. And Sila saw he was smiling big.

Gio hired two more people to help at his property. A man named Carlos Flores came five days a week and was placed in charge of managing the enormous amount of hay that Veda ate. He also was put to work planting a garden in a flat area at the top of the hill behind the farmhouse. Sila and Mateo spent part of every day now tending the new seedlings. There were vegetables and sunflowers that had just started to grow there.

Gio's second full-time worker was named Klay Roker. He helped the kids collect Veda's potent poo, most of which was hauled away on schedule twice a week and sold as fertilizer at a nursery in town. Carlos and Klay tried to keep Gio from doing too much of the heavy work. Each morning when the kids arrived they were given an assignment. Some days they would join Gio in the afternoon to watch Veda. Other times after they had helped in the barn, they were allowed to climb trees or explore the woods. On one hike they found a small cave. They went back with Gio and flashlights, but there wasn't treasure inside, just dripping water and a lot of spiders.

Gio taught Sila and Mateo to drive the golf cart, which had a trailer that could be attached to transport food and other equipment around the property. They learned to use saws and power tools. They were always busy, and even when the work for the day was tiring or repetitive, it felt great to be outside near the majestic elephant.

32.

It was on a Sunday night at the end of June when Gio phoned Alp to say there were friends for Veda arriving the next day. The kids should try to get to his place early.

Sila asked, "What's his definition of friends?"

Her father shrugged. "I guess you'll see."

The kids had only been on the property for five minutes before the buzzer at the gate rang. Gio called out from the front porch of the farmhouse, "They're here!"

Sila and Mateo exchanged looks, anxious to know who "they" were as the gates rolled open and a cargo van pulled in. A curly-haired man got out. He looked both energized and weary. It was a strange combination.

Gio extended his hand. "I'm Gio. You must be Pip Rozaire."

"That's me. I've been on the road for twenty hours. Stopped just for gas and to go to the bathroom. I was trying to give the phenicopters as little grief as possible."

Sila stared at him. Phenicopters? She'd been making a to-do list for the day and was holding a pad of paper. She wrote down the word *phenicopters* and put a question mark next to it.

Pip opened the back of the transport vehicle, and the kids and Gio looked in to see blankets covering large dog crates. Sila thought it was strange that Gio would buy a bunch of dogs, but then the man pulled the cover off a crate and inside, sitting on a pile of shredded, damp towels, was a flamingo.

The bird was jittery. So was Pip Rozaire, who for some reason addressed most of what he said to Sila. Maybe because she had the paper and pen.

"The biggest thing you're going to need is a lot of sand. And you've got to be prepared to water that sand a few times a day."

She wrote, *We need lots of sand. Water it.*

Pip continued, "Otherwise, big problem. It's wet sand they want. Now remember, flamingos can get their legs hurt pretty darn easily. They trip all the time. Real klutzes. And if something scares 'em, they take off running. When that happens, their legs tangle up and can even break. Flamingos with broken legs—not pretty. Exotic vet bills are not cheap. I hope there's an exotic bird veterinarian around here. We have two in Vegas."

Sila wrote down: *Find exotic bird vet. Flamingos are real klutzes.*

Gio sounded alarmed. "Exotic bird vet? I didn't know about that. I guess I should have done more flamingo research."

Mateo spoke. "Did you do any flamingo research?"

Gio didn't answer.

Mateo kept looking at him.

"Before I go to bed I read about different places in Africa and Asia where there are elephants," Gio told him.

Mateo persisted. "You're reading books or articles?"

Sila thought Gio looked caught. He said, "Mostly I look at pictures online. And a few days ago I saw a beautiful photo of an elephant in water surrounded by flamingos. So I looked to see if I could buy a few."

Pip Rozaire smiled at Sila and Mateo. "And he found me. In Las Vegas. It was fate."

The crates weren't heavy since the largest flamingo only weighed eight pounds. They all helped get the birds out of the van and onto the ground next to the farmhouse porch.

Mr. Rozaire was in charge. "I'm going to open the doors. They're shy at first. And they've been cooped up for twenty hours. So expect 'em to be dullards."

He removed the locks on the crates and opened the doors.

Not a single flamingo moved. They stayed as still as their plastic lawn ornament counterparts. Then one bird lifted its long, pink neck, and a pair of eyes on a head with a boomerang-shaped, black-tipped beak appeared in the open door of the crate.

Eventually all eight flamingos had their necks extended and their heads out. And then it was like a pool table when the cue ball hits the triangle. The birds exploded out of the plastic crates. The flamingos were eager to be free of the cramped cages and in open space, but they also seemed confused and very rattled at what they found. This was an open space the likes of which they had never seen.

Mr. Rozaire went to the van and came back with a pair of shears. He handed them to Gio, who in turn passed them straight to Sila. She gave them to Mateo. He seemed interested in the sharp tool. Pip went on to explain, "Those are feather clippers. Flamingos fly, so you're going to have to keep the wing feathers cut. Really a two-person job. You'll need a big blanket to make the catch. And be prepared for a lot of running. When you've got the bird under your control one person holds it down wrapped in the blanket. Then the other person pulls out a wing and does the snip-snip. Think of it like cutting toenails. It has to be done."

Sila found her voice. "How often?"

Pip Rozaire was facing her now. "I'm going to say once a month. This group is close to needing a whack."

Mateo looked from the clippers he was holding to the birds, and tried to pass the tool back to Gio.

Pip continued, "If you don't want to do the clippy-clip, you've got the choice of the full pinion."

Mateo's eyes flashed with something Sila read as dismay. "What's a pinion?" he asked. Sila had no idea either.

"Son, that's a fancy word for cutting off a chunk of a bird's wing."

Sila felt her hand, which was holding her notepad, go weak as he continued. "They can't fly after the pinion. *Obviously* don't try doing that yourself. Get the exotic vet involved. It's an operation—surgery is what I'm saying. I didn't pinion. But that's how most zoos handle flamingos. Least that's what I been told. It was too pricey for me to consider."

Gio had been quiet, but not anymore. "We're not cutting off half their wings!"

Sila looked over at Mateo. They were both relieved.

"Up to you. They're your birds now."

Mr. Rozaire pulled a wad of rolled-up papers from out of his back pocket and gave them to Gio.

"Here you go. Instructions on care and feeding. Also, there's a release. You need to sign that. I'm turning them over to you. No returns. No liability."

Sila realized the man's face was wet with perspiration. And it wasn't hot out. He looked right at her and said, "Here's some advice: Don't renovate a motel if your marriage isn't strong. Also, think twice about calling any place in Las Vegas 'The Other Flamingo.'"

Sila nodded and asked the only question at this point that she cared about. "Do the birds have names?"

It was a cloudy day, but Pip Rozaire squinted up into the sky as if he was looking into bright light. He finally said, "The biggest one is Pink Floyd. But they don't come when you call 'em, so you can give 'em any name you want."

Once Gio had signed the paper he wanted, the man climbed back in his van and started the engine, not even going to the bathroom or taking the cup of coffee Gio offered. "You said you've got a pond. They're filter-feeders. You can read up on that. It means they scoop water and sift through it for food."

He then put the vehicle in reverse and almost ran over a flamingo. He honked the horn of the truck, which sent the birds off in eight different directions. The flamingos were faster on their feet than they looked. And he was right, they were klutzes.

Right away the birds found something of great interest. It wasn't the water Gio had put out. Or the pile of fresh fruit, or the blankets and cushions. It was Veda's poop. The birds ran to the mound behind the barn and began pecking wildly at the waste material.

Gio shouted, "Are they eating it?"

"I'm not sure," said Sila. "But Mr. Gio, I bet the first person to called someone a 'birdbrain' had spent time with flamingos."

33.

It took more than two hours to get the eight flamingos down to the pond. It was like herding cats. Or like herding flamingos. In the end, Gio drove the golf cart slowly down the dirt road while Sila and Mateo held ropes with bags of Veda poo tied to the ends.

Sila saw Veda watch as a parade of flamingos approached. Her expression seemed to say, "Well, this is interesting." When the flamingos got to the pond they went right to it. Whenever the elephant moved in the direction of the birds, they scattered.

Sila whispered, "It hardly feels like the basis for a friendship."

Eventually Veda got out of the water. The beginning of some kind of bond formed when she dropped one of her turds onto the muddy shore. The flamingos rushed to check it out. Sila figured they would soon make the connection between the smelly material and the maker of such gifts.

Mateo noted, "Well, maybe they'll come to appreciate what they each have to offer."

For the flamingos, it would probably always be the fresh turds. But Sila liked to believe that for Veda, it might be the grace of a living creature with legs so thin and a neck so long. Anyone, she thought, could see that the construction of a flamingo was a marvel.

Sila, Mateo, and Gio sat in the golf cart and watched as the birds began taking apart elephant droppings, working to build what looked like large traffic cones. The flamingos toiled away independently, but all the while checking one another's progress. The birds had a method to their madness. It wasn't long before each flamingo had a version of a dung nest positioned on the pond's shoreline. When they perched on their nests the tops smashed and the structures resembled small volcanoes. It was a sight to see for all involved.

The birds were busy creatures. After making the nests, they went back into the water, as Pip Rozaire had said, and began an activity that Sila later discovered would always take up the bulk of their day. The flamingos scooped water into their beaks, which were reversed from a regular bird beak, and then sifted through the liquid for food, most of which was too small to even see. They spit out the rest.

After watching how they operated, Sila told Gio, "I guess they're spitting all the time, only it just looks like they have drippy beaks."

Mateo was reading the papers Mr. Rozaire had left behind. "They're eating algae."

This seemed to make Gio happy. "There's plenty of that out there."

"It says here that their rate of filtration is twenty times a minute."

Mateo handed the paperwork to Sila, who read out loud, "A group of flamingos is called a pat."

Two of the flamingos appeared to be skimming the top of the water. Mateo, sounding fascinated, said, "I think they're eating mosquitoes."

Gio seemed thrilled. "Have at it."

Veda shook her head from side to side, and Sila proclaimed, "She likes them!"

"Or maybe she doesn't like mosquitoes," said Mateo.

Sila rode her bike home that afternoon with Mateo filled with a new understanding of flamingos. They were pedaling slowly on the side of the road when she observed, "Once you know about something, you see it differently. I'll never look at the pink plastic flamingos people stick on their lawns the same way again."

Mateo nodded in agreement, adding, "That's why it's a good idea to read the ingredients on packaging."

Sila was confused. "What do you mean?"

"There's always something inside that you're not seeing."

She wasn't sure she understood completely. Later she found herself wondering if maybe he was talking about himself.

That night Sila's voice was filled with enthusiasm as she told her father about her day. This was something that had been mostly missing since Oya had left, and only the elephant and Gio brought it back. Sila explained, "It looks like the flamingos are just standing around, but they're good swimmers. They glide into the deep part of the pond with their pink heads skimming the top of the water."

"I can't wait to meet these birds," Alp said.

"I wish Mom could see."

Sila regretted her words as soon as she said them. Of course she wished that. And so did her dad. But now the empty chair across from Sila looked even emptier. Alp got up from the table to clear the plates. They no longer used the dishwasher. Neither of them knew why. Instead they rinsed the same two plates, two forks, and two knives every day, and put them on the rack to dry. Oya used the dishwasher. Did three people make that much more of a mess than two? It made no sense. But so many things in their lives now didn't.

The next day proved that Pip Rozaire was right: The flamingos could fly. The eight birds were down to only five by the time the kids arrived on the property. One flew south to a Courtyard Marriott, where guests were thrilled to wake up and find a flamingo in the swimming pool. Sila read about it in the local paper. A cemetery four miles east had a big, broken fountain with lily pads and all kinds of green slime that attracted two of the escapees. Gio told Sila he'd gotten word of the graveyard birds but hadn't gone to retrieve them because the groundskeeper reported that the first mourners to arrive found the flamingos comforting in their time of grief. But the five who didn't fly away seemed to really like Gio's place. A lot. Maybe they understood there wasn't anywhere better for them within striking distance.

That morning Gio had gotten on the phone with the local gravel company and ordered truckloads of fine sand, which by midday was dumped around Veda's pond. The flamingos weren't rocket scientists, but they could see that the new powdery stuff was better than Veda's poop, so they started building with the sand.

Gio's next call had been to the local nursery. He bought water lilies, marsh marigolds, pickerel rush, sedges, and cattails, and hired the nursery workers to plant them. Sila and Mateo helped.

Minnow eggs were ordered, along with crayfish. Gio told Sila and Mateo that he'd read that in order to stay pink, the birds needed to have crustaceans in their diet. As it turned out, there were fairy shrimp already living in the pond. Sila and Mateo discovered this that evening when they put drops of the water on a slide to view under Mateo's microscope. This close-up work was Mateo's favorite thing to do once he was home from a day at Gio's. He and Sila filled a bottle with pond water and he carried it home in his backpack. Suddenly Sila felt like a scientist.

Sila's favorite time of every day at Gio's was with Veda. She had come to see that there was a lot to understand about elephant behavior. Veda used her trunk to put mud on her back, which was to protect her skin. It was sunscreen in the form of mud-screen. The elephant also used tools, often taking a branch in her trunk and holding it like a flyswatter to slap at insects.

But today Sila learned one of the most remarkable things Veda could do: imitate the sound of the brakes on the golf cart. At first they'd all thought they were hearing things. But then Sila realized that Veda had made the same mechanical brake sound as the cart when they stopped at the crest of the hill.

"She's a parrot," Gio said.

Sila answered, "No, she's smarter than that. She's an elephant, and they are the most amazing creatures in the world."

Down at the pond, Sila stood next to Veda watching as two flamingos pushed sand and mud around on the shore. She whispered softly to the elephant, "Flamingos have strong ideas about nests." Veda leaned forward, touching the girl with her trunk. Sila kissed her leathery skin and whispered, "The birds are pretty, but you are everything."

34.

It was while sitting in the golf cart at the pond two weeks after the flamingos arrived that Gio asked, "Sila? You're so quiet. Is everything okay?"

She shrugged.

"Come on. Tell me."

"Today's my mom's birthday."

Gio understood immediately. "I'm sorry, sweetheart."

"I'll talk to her tonight before I go to bed. It's ten hours later there. It will be morning for her. But still her birthday here."

"She will love that."

Sila mumbled, "I wonder when Veda was born. And where."

"The man said she was young when he got her. Not even two years old."

Sila's voice was back to being not much more than a whisper. "Where do you think her mother and father are now?"

"I don't know, Sila."

But the idea of Veda's family suddenly animated Sila. "What about in the papers the circus guy left? Is there anything there that explains?"

Gio offered, "You could take a look at that notebook Chester gave me."

Later when Mateo was working with Klay and Carlos, Gio suggested going to get the black notebook that Chester had left. Every day Sila was in the farmhouse to use the bathroom or get something from the refrigerator, but she never went into the living room or lingered inside for any length of time. Today was different. Gio directed her to a bookcase.

Sila was eager to take a look, but her eyes fell on three shelves of identical binders. Gio noticed. "Those were put together by my wife. She made one for every year she taught school."

Sila scanned the spines on the shelf and saw the year when she'd had Mrs. Gardino as her second-grade teacher. Then she heard Gio add, "Go ahead. Take a look if you want."

Sila wasn't sure why she felt butterflies in her stomach when she pulled the binder with her year from the shelf. She took a seat on the couch and turned to the first page, where she saw the official picture of her whole class. She had her own copy of this photograph, but it felt different looking at it here. So much had changed. Mrs. Gardino was gone. Sila's mom had been overseas for months and months. Sila looked at her own smiling image and realized she had a tooth missing back then. Sila seemed so little in the picture. But also so happy.

Her eyes landed next on Mateo. He was in the back row all the way over on the left side. He had on a bow tie. Sila wondered what he'd been thinking about that day.

She turned the page and saw a typed list with the names of all the kids and their parents next to email addresses and lots of phone numbers. After this there was a school calendar, a picture of the class in Halloween costumes, and then a printed program for the holiday assembly. There were three pages of Valentines, and the largest one was from Mateo. He had filled an entire page with stick-on hearts.

What followed were photos from a field trip to a fish hatchery in March and an event in April called "Touch a Truck," which was put on by the city recreation center. Sila was surprised to see the menu from the cafeteria for a single week in May. Why had Mrs. Gardino kept that? The food didn't look very interesting. Was that the point?

The final pages were drawings that students had made

throughout the year. One of Mateo's drawings of Waffles was in the book. He was a puppy in the picture, and she wasn't sure it was the same dog until she saw *Good dog Waffles* written in small print at the bottom of the piece of paper.

Sila was sad to see Mrs. Gardino hadn't saved any of her work. She felt doubly bad because there were *three* pictures done by Paloma Casaroli. Sila took a long look at the three drawings and had to admit that Paloma was a really good artist.

Finally Sila turned to the last page of the binder. A poem had been glued to the paper. She stared at the words and read:

MY TEACHER

Is redee every mornning even if I am not.

My Teacher

Shows me how to thingk hard and lurn a lot.

My Teacher

Fills my hart with love

More than she will ever no.

My Teacher

Is named Lillian Gardino

And I will miss her next yere

But also for ever.

Sila Tekin age 7 (Sorry I kood not find a word that is
good with for ever)

Under the poem in Lillian Gardino's lovely handwriting Sila saw the words: "The sweetest little girl in the world."

"You can keep that binder," Gio told her.

Sila was holding it tightly to her chest. Her fingers gripped the edges hard. She hadn't shown Gio the poem, and she didn't know if he realized it was inside.

"Are you sure?"

"Yes. It's yours now."

"Really? Thank you. Thank you so much."

"My wife would have wanted you to have it."

For a single moment, just a slice of a second, it felt to Sila as if Lillian Gardino was in the room. Generations of people who had come before her were also there, unknown and unseen but holding her up, giving her both air and light and room to breathe.

And then Gio broke the spell and said, "Let's see where I put that stuff about Veda."

Sila's backpack was heavier than usual as she pedaled home. Inside was not just the prized binder, but also the notebook Chester had given Gio. Once she and Mateo were in town she realized she had no memory of the ride through the countryside or even on the busy highway. She had disappeared inside her head and was thinking of the classroom where she had once sat by the window. She didn't feel as sad now. Her mother's birthday and Mrs. Gardino's words had intertwined in a hopeful way.

And for that Sila was grateful.

Gio had looked at the binder. More than once. He had read Sila's poem and he had been waiting for the right time to show her. He didn't want Mateo to feel left out, but also, if he were honest with himself, he would have had to admit that it wasn't easy to let go of anything that had been so connected to his wife.

With the kids gone for the day, Veda back in the barn, and the flamingos preening down at the pond, he sat down in the chair by the window and watched the hills in the distance fade from gold to a purplish gray. He was glad that

Sila had his wife's school year memories. In difficult times, thinking about the past could be a savior for him. But since Sila and Mateo and Veda were in his life, he could also find comfort in the future.

It belonged to them.

35.

Sila was at the kitchen table on the computer with a notebook open when her father came home. He moved closer to see her looking down at a yellowy slip of paper.

"I'm doing research. This is a receipt from when Veda was sold twenty-one years ago. It says she's two years old. So that means Veda is almost twenty-three years old."

Alp read from the paper, "Vincent Z. Doyle Enterprises."

"That's the man who sold her. What's great is he doesn't have a common name. If his name was Bob Smith it would make finding out stuff so much harder."

Her father nodded but he had already started out of the room to change from his work clothes. Sila returned to the computer. Locating Vincent Z. Doyle felt like a birthday present. Maybe not for her mother, but on Cleary Road it seemed to her like something to celebrate.

Just down the street, Mateo was staring down at his dinner plate. If he had a choice in the matter, and he didn't, he

would eat macaroni and cheese every night. And today he was getting his favorite meal. As he put his fork into his food he was pleased. After almost two hours riding a bicycle and six hours outside at Gio's property, Mateo was hungry.

His mother slid into the chair next to him. "Anything new to report from Gio's today?"

"Sila wished she had never kicked the hornet's nest."

Rosa looked up with concern. "Goodness—was she stung?"

"No."

"Well, I'm glad to hear it. Kicking a hornet's nest is very dangerous."

"I didn't see it happen. Today is her mom's birthday. She said it's her fault her mom got sent back to Turkey because she kicked the hornet's nest."

"Why would that be her fault?"

"She looked at a paycheck from the hotel where her mom worked and she saw that the janitors got more money than the maids, so her mom complained to her boss."

Rosa stopped eating. "I don't understand what you're saying."

"They fired her mom after she complained about the check. Then immigration wrote and said there was a problem. Sila seeing the paycheck started a chain of bad stuff."

"Oh. I get it. Sila saying she kicked the hornet's nest is just an expression."

"An expression of what?" Mateo asked.

"Trouble."

"Really?"

"Yes. I don't think hornets are connected in any way to the immigration problem."

"Sila should have said that."

Mateo's mother was no longer eating. She looked at her son. "I wondered what was going on with Sila's mother. But I didn't think it was right to ask a lot of personal questions."

"People don't like answering a lot of questions," Mateo agreed.

"Do they have a good lawyer?" Rosa asked.

"For what?"

"For the problem."

"I don't know."

"I need to speak with Sila's father."

Mateo served himself more macaroni and cheese. He ate for a while. When he was finished he took his plate to the kitchen, saying over his shoulder, "Mom, bees and hornets get blamed for a lot of stuff they don't do."

Sila was already in her room in bed, but she heard the doorbell ring. She was able to make out bits and pieces of a conversation between her father and Mateo's mother.

"Alp, I'm not an immigration lawyer. My specialty is labor law. But there's a lawyer in our firm who does immigration."

Sila put her ear to the wall to listen. Her father answered, "We can't hire anyone right now."

"No, you don't understand. This won't cost anything. It would be pro bono."

What did *pro bono* mean? Sila slipped out of bed and quickly typed the words into her computer and read: "*Pro bono publico* is a Latin phrase for work done as a volunteer without payment."

Well, that had to be good news.

Sila waited. There was silence. Then she heard Mrs. Lopez's voice:

"I want to help. I'd really like to look at the documents you've received from the government. And find out more about what happened at the hotel."

Sila couldn't understand what her father said in reply.

But then she heard him pass down the hallway outside her room. Before long he was back at the front door.

"This is from the hotel. And these are from Citizenship and Immigration Services."

Sila had never seen whatever he was showing Mrs. Lopez. She heard her say, "I'll make copies of everything and get this back to you tomorrow."

Sila couldn't see her father, but in her mind's eye she could imagine him standing in the doorway with his face in shadow and his body in silhouette, looking defeated.

Then Rosa Lopez, sounding to Sila as if she was forcing herself to be optimistic, said, "Let me see what I can do."

Back at home, Mateo's mother cleaned the kitchen and then went to tell her son it was bedtime. These days she no longer had to argue with him about turning off a game console or putting down a book. By the time she made it upstairs she could hear Mateo snoring even with his door half shut. That's what all the bike riding and outdoor work had done. He was exhausted at the end of the day.

Rosa changed into pajamas and propped herself up on pillows in bed. She started through the letters in the file Alp had given her, noting that the Tekins had entered the country legally fourteen years ago. They had come seeking political asylum. Alp's father was Kurdish, a cultural minority in Turkey. He had been politically active and had been jailed as a dissident. Oya was not Kurdish, and part of the reason they had left the country was to start a new life together free from the political struggle. They picked Oregon because they had heard it was very green and that people were friendly and welcoming. They had established a life in the Willamette Valley.

The Tekins had applied for lawful permanent resident status, and after a number of steps, which included submission of evidence and supporting documentation, they each received Social Security numbers and visas. They had both found jobs and paid taxes. But Oya's permission to work was issued as a temporary document. Alp's was not. He was the asylum seeker. Her classification was as a spouse.

Rosa was no expert in immigration law. But she knew that the situation had recently changed for people coming from Muslim countries. Sila Tekin was born in America and was a citizen. So she didn't have a problem. But Oya was the spouse of an asylum seeker. Spouses no longer received the same protection under the law as they had fourteen years ago.

After reading the contents of the file, Rosa took her laptop from the night table and sent Alp an email asking questions about his wife's job at the Grand Hotel. Alp answered immediately. Only two months before Oya was let go, she had been named hotel Employee of the Month. She was always on time. She had a good attitude. She did exactly what the hotel wanted her to do. At least, until the morning she had gone to speak about the differences in pay in the employment of men and women who cleaned the hotel.

That night when Rosa had arrived at his apartment, Alp Tekin had been angry, afraid, and suspicious. The system didn't seem to him to be fair. Alp's words were simple: "I came to this country because it was a place to start a new life. I have a degree as a mechanical engineer. Here in America I work as an automotive mechanic. It's not the same thing, but my wife and I have been very happy. Our daughter was born. We felt so fortunate. But now my family's situation is broken. And it's not like a bad truck engine. I don't have the parts to fix this problem."

It was late when Rosa closed her computer. She turned off the table lamp but remained sitting up in bed. The room was at first totally dark. As her eyes adjusted she began to make out the furniture in the room. And then gradually the light from a sliver of moon glowing through the window allowed her to see what was really there. Two things were going on: Oya Tekin had a serious immigration issue. But Oya Tekin also had a grievance for wrongful employment termination from the hotel. She had the making of a workplace retaliation lawsuit. Were her firing and the immigration problem connected? Or was it all just a terrible coincidence?

36.

I t was Sunday, which was the only morning Sila and Mateo didn't bike out to Gio's. Sila got up early and walked six blocks to Mateo's house. She carried Chester's notebook along with the information she'd written down about Vincent Z. Doyle. Mateo was sitting on the porch with his dog, waiting for her. She took a seat next to them.

"Your mom came over last night to talk to my dad."

"I heard."

"She said she's going to help my parents. Pro bono." Sila was waiting to tell him what that meant. Instead Mateo answered, "Pro bono publico. Latin 'for the good of the people.'"

She couldn't help but be irritated that he already knew this. She thought she finally might know something he didn't. "Right."

"She does a bunch of cases like that." He looked at the notebook in her hands. "Did you find out anything about Veda?"

"Yeah. The guy listed on the bill of sale was an exotic animal broker in Chicago."

"That sounds like an interesting job. I wonder how you train for that."

"It's not as exciting as it sounds. It looks like all he did was arrange to have animals moved."

"He has a website?"

"No. He had an obituary."

"So he's dead?"

"He is."

"Did it say what kinds of animals he moved?"

Sila opened her notebook and read: "Elephants, hippos, sugar gliders, squirrels, chinchillas, lions, and even 'large quantities of insects.'"

"What kinds of insects are shipped in large quantities?" Mateo asked. He then sounded hopeful: "Bees?"

"It didn't say."

Mateo then went off on a tangent. "I had an ant farm once. But after two months the ants all died. It wasn't a farm, obviously. It was two pieces of clear plastic with sand in between. You order the ants separately and they come in the mail. The ants eat sugar water at first. Then half a grape can last them a whole week. My mom was happy when they died and I had to throw it all out. I'm not sure if I fed them too much or too little."

Mateo stared intently at the ground and Sila decided he was now looking for ants.

"Anyway, Vincent Z. Doyle's obituary said he died six years ago at Highland Park Hospital in Illinois at the age of eighty-one."

"Did he get crushed loading a rhinoceros into a crate?"

"It said natural causes."

"Which covers a lot," said Mateo.

"We have the name of his business."

"We should call them."

"It closed when he died. Maybe it wasn't much more than him. But we're on the trail."

Mateo's eyes were back on the ground. "When ants find food, a chemical comes out of their bodies. We can't see it. But other ants smell it and follow. Then every ant that walks the same path releases the same chemical. That's why they move in lines in such an organized way."

"Well, that's good to know. Thanks." Sila was teasing him. But sometimes Mateo couldn't tell the difference between her being sincere and snarky.

"You're welcome."

They left the ants behind and went inside to continue the investigation. The obituary said Vincent Z. Doyle was survived by a daughter named Penny. So they searched for a person named Penny Doyle. But it turned out there were many people online named Penny Doyle. There was a food writer. A gymnast. Realtors in different parts of the country. There were multiple Penny Doyles in Illinois. But it was while looking up Penny Doyle that they came upon an interview done in *The Kenosha News* children's page in Wisconsin, which was where Vincent Z. Doyle and his family must have spent a vacation one summer. This small newspaper had a column that mentioned kids from out of the area. It said: "Penny Doyle and her family are up from Chicago. Penny's father works with such interesting clients as the Larmen and Falls Circus as he moves animals. Penny has quite a few stories to tell."

Sila was excited. "We know Veda was sold to the man named Chester. We know Vincent Z. Doyle arranged it. And now we have the circus where she might have come from."

Mateo searched Larmen and Falls, and read aloud from the computer screen: "For over seventy-five years the circus traveled with all sorts of animals and performers, setting up a three-ring show in small towns and big cities across North America." He stopped reading. "So Veda might have been born in that circus and sold to another smaller one."

"And Vincent Z. Doyle did the moving."

"We need to research circuses."

Sila shot him a look. "I think we need to concentrate just on Larmen and Falls."

But Mateo was already in command of the keyboard, typing. Sila took notes from what he said. She wrote on her pad of paper:

In 1808 a man named HACHALIAH BAILEY somehow bought one of the first elephants to come to America (from India). Supposedly the idea behind Mr. Bailey's purchase was to have the elephant plow his field instead of a horse. It feels like everyone back then was a farmer.

Only plowing the fields for Mr. Bailey didn't work out because the elephant ATE TOO MUCH FOOD and also the elephant didn't really want to act like a horse.

But people came from all around the area to get a look at Hachaliah Bailey's elephant, so he started charging 25¢ a person to see her. In order to collect the money, he had a BIG CURTAIN made and he hid the elephant until everyone waiting in line had paid. He ended up making a set time during the day for the PERFORMANCE, which was when the curtain was pulled back and people got to see the elephant. Today Mr. Bailey is considered the father of American circuses. He died when a horse kicked him in the head, which is ironic.

At 12:08 p.m. Mrs. Lopez put out tuna sandwiches, almonds, and chips, and Sila and Mateo took a short break. The bad news was that Larmen and Falls had gone out of business, citing "the high cost of running the operation and a failure to find audiences."

While eating, Sila asked Mateo, "Have you ever been to a circus?"

"No. Unless I don't remember because I was really little. What about you?"

"Same," Sila said.

"They're mostly all closed now."

"Which I think is a good thing."

Mateo carefully counted out seven almonds as Sila continued, "Maybe circuses aren't popular today because we have TV and movies and YouTube to watch animals and people perform. When circuses were really popular, there weren't so many choices."

Mateo stopped chewing his almonds. "Maybe if we didn't have so many choices it would be better. One of the reasons I have the same lunch every day is that otherwise there are too many variables."

Sila nodded. She could see his point. When she liked something, she stuck with it. The modern world had a lot of options.

After they finished eating they went right back to work. The good news was they discovered that even though Larmen and Falls was out of business, their website was still up. It explained that the company's elephants had all been relocated to sanctuaries, mostly one in Florida.

This was a big breakthrough. Sila and Mateo were able to find the Florida sanctuary, and they wrote a letter.

Dear Elephant Sanctuary People,

Our names are Sila Tekin and Mateo Lopez. We live in

Oregon and we work (as paid interns) for a man named Giovanni Gardino. He bought an elephant named VEDA from a man named Chester Briot. Chester Briot ran the Briot Family Circus. He bought this elephant from Vincent Z. Doyle, a wild animal broker in Chicago. According to our research he did a lot of work for Larmen and Falls.

We know about this because we have the bill of sale for Veda, which is from twenty-one years ago.

You should know that today Veda is living a very good life in Oregon.

Attached to this email is a picture of the paperwork. We're keeping the original because it goes in a notebook that doesn't belong to us.

We are writing because we are hoping you can tell us if Veda came from the Larmen and Falls circus, and if she did, where Veda's mother or father or other elephants such as sisters or brothers are today.

Family is very important. For people, but also for animals in the world.

It is a fact that the six animals with very important family structures are: Elephants. Wolves. Orca whales. Dolphins. Lions. And chimpanzees. We didn't make up the list. It is in one of Mateo's science books.

Thank you for your help. And thank you for caring about animals.

Sincerely, Sila Tekin & Mateo Lopez

P.S. We are sending this as an email, but we decided that we are printing out a copy of this letter and sending it the old-fashioned way with a stamp and an envelope. Many people don't open email from strangers, but everyone opens a letter (we hope).

37.

Rosa Lopez made copies of everything Alp Tekin had given her, and sent it to her friend who was a specialist in immigration law. Then she started investigating Oya's former employment situation at the Grand Hotel.

From what she knew, Oya Tekin had done nothing wrong as an employee. Many people believed you could sue if you were fired unfairly. But that wasn't true. A law needed to have been broken in order to have a legitimate wrongful termination claim.

Rosa knew that there weren't laws against a boss liking one employee better than another. However, there was a law called the Equal Pay Act to guarantee that women couldn't do the same job as men and be paid less.

Rosa had been standing up for her son to receive accommodations in school because of his differences, and so she was used to fighting for people's rights. She began by immediately filling out paperwork on behalf of Oya Tekin to open

a case with the United States Equal Employment Opportunity Commission. While they started an official investigation, she then went one step further. She started the motions to file a case against the hotel.

The ball was rolling.

Rosa called Alp at work to let him know. She needed signatures from Oya, and they arranged a time for the women to speak. Rosa and Alp made the decision not to tell either Sila or Mateo any of the details. Bringing up all of the immigration problems seemed to only make both kids more anxious. They would let them know when there was real news to report. In the meantime, it was enough for the kids to be told that lawyers were now working for the Tekin family.

Sila checked her email six times that day, but there was no reply from Florida. On Monday she and Mateo rode their bikes back out to Gio's, but didn't mention the search or sending the message to the sanctuary.

There was no response on Monday, or Tuesday or Wednesday. On Thursday Sila re-sent the email with a new subject heading: SENDING THIS EMAIL A SECOND TIME HOPING PLEASE PLEASE PLEASE FOR AN ANSWER.

Two days later there was a reply!

Sila and Mateo,

My name is Annie Byrd and I work at the Elephant Sanctuary Center of West Florida (ESCWF). I'm sorry it took several days for me to answer your email. I get a lot of correspondence at the sanctuary, which is forwarded to me from the general information website.

One of the things that we have been working on here is a database for all the animals that were owned by Larmen and Falls. We are very close to having a full history. Of course, many of the elephants are no longer living. But every elephant that was once part of the show is now retired. Most are in Florida, only not all.

I was able to see that a female elephant was born during the time period that you asked about and named Veda, which is a Sanskrit word meaning "knowledge and wisdom." This was probably given to her because their elephants were Indian, not African. The birth of the baby elephant was considered a wonderful event for the circus, and there is documentation in the Santa Fe newspaper (where the circus was located for part of that winter). The records for the circus show that when the elephant calf was twenty months old she was sold through Vincent Z. Doyle. So this would confirm she is the same elephant you tell us is in Oregon.

The mother of Veda is named Madhi, and she is one of the few elephants from Larmen and Falls that did not end up here in the Florida sanctuary. Madhi is living in Arizona. A company called Arizona Outdoor Wildlife Adventures, run by the Randolf family, is a sanctuary that is also a commercial business operating for animal viewing.

The father of your elephant was Paya. He died of natural causes four years ago here in Florida.

We are very glad to have this news of Veda and we will add it to her life story. Thank you for your inquiry and for your interest in elephants from the Larmen and Falls Circus.

Best regards,
Annie Byrd
Elephant Sanctuary Center of West Florida

"She's in Arizona!" Sila exclaimed as soon as Mateo came out of his house.

"Who's in Arizona?"

"Madhi's in Arizona!"

"Oh."

Then Mateo asked, "Who's Madhi?"

"Veda's mother. I want to go see her."

"In Arizona?"

"Yes! Do you think we could talk to your mom? Do you think she'd want to do that?"

"Go to Arizona?"

"Yes!"

"To see an elephant?"

"Not just any elephant. Madhi. Veda's mother!"

"You said that already." Mateo thought for a moment. "No. I don't think my mom wants to go to Arizona. She's never expressed an interest in that. She said she wants to go to Paris."

"You haven't even asked!" Sila shouted.

"Your question was 'do you think she would?' It wasn't 'do you think you could ask her?'"

"Mateo, you're not seeing the big picture!"

"You have a picture? I'd like to look at it."

"Mateo, please."

"Please what?"

Sila slumped into the handlebars of her bicycle. Mateo looked concerned. "Are you okay to ride out to Gio's this morning?"

She realized she shouldn't have jumped into conversation that way. She needed to stay in order, and not just when talking to Mateo. She hadn't explained about the email from the sanctuary. By the time they reached Gio's, she had figured out a different way to share the news.

"Gio, we found Veda's mother. She's in Arizona. We have an email from a woman who works for the sanctuary that takes care of the elephants from the circus where Veda was born."

"Goodness," Gio said. "You two are real detectives."

"Technically we're not," Mateo answered. "We weren't solving a crime."

Sila piped up, "Unless you see all circuses with trained animals as a crime."

Mateo looked from Sila to Gio. "In 1808 a farmer named Hachaliah Bailey bought one of the first elephants to be shipped to America. He wanted to have an elephant pull a plow instead of a horse."

Gio looked intrigued. "I didn't know that."

Sila knew it was wrong to interrupt but worried that an in-depth history discussion was coming. She blurted out, "Veda's mother is now in an animal sanctuary in Arizona. That's what we found out!"

Gio's head ping-ponged from Mateo to Sila. "You're kidding!"

Mateo returned to what he wanted to share. "But the elephant ate too much and didn't like pulling the plow."

Gio told Sila he couldn't take her and Mateo on a trip to Arizona. He didn't feel comfortable leaving Veda, even though Carlos and Klay knew how to feed her and how to watch over the flamingos. He was interested in hearing more about the elephants in Veda's family, but he didn't share the kids' strong enthusiasm to see Madhi in person. Right now, he said, "he had his hands full."

Sila tried not to show how disappointed she was.

She was used to hiding her feelings, or at least she thought she was.

38.

Time was endless when Sila was thinking about how long it had been since she'd seen her mother. But the summer days had passed at lightning speed. July was behind them. August was almost over. School was about to start. Spending the day at Gio's would soon be in the past. Sila and Mateo wouldn't ride bikes or push wheelbarrows. They wouldn't drive the golf cart (they were experts now), or water sunflowers or pull weeds in the pumpkin patch with Carlos and Klay. They wouldn't watch hawks soar overhead or see an elephant in a pond, showering herself with muddy water as insects buzzed in frenzied circles. They wouldn't watch Veda call out to them when they arrived, stomping her feet with excitement and splashing the pond. Sila and Mateo wouldn't eat tuna fish sandwiches together on the front porch of a farmhouse with a kind older man who loved bright colors, elephants, and them.

Before long the Oregon rain would descend with numbing frequency. Sila knew there was a reason, after all, that

this part of the country was so green. The pines would hold on to their needles, but the other trees would change color, and leaves would drop to the muddy ground below. The longest day of summer in the Willamette Valley had nearly sixteen hours of sunlight. The shortest winter day had not much more than eight.

Winter would bring frost and icy morning roads and, on a handful of occasions, snow. Gio had paid to have the old barn insulated and heating installed in preparation for when Veda might not want to go out into the cold weather. For the first time Sila wanted time to slow down, not speed up.

Sila's father spent the weekend before school started cleaning the apartment, organizing everything in their lives in a kind of frenzy that Sila found irritating. Didn't he see how unhappy she was? It wasn't just that she waited every day and every night to hear her mother's voice. The problem was supposed to have been solved long ago, and now that the joy of the summer was behind her she didn't know if she could stand it anymore. She knew money was tight but wished her father had taken her to a movie, or out for ice cream. Instead he'd bought a new mop at Home Depot and put wax on the kitchen floor. He asked if she wanted to get a haircut, and when she said no, he went and got one for himself. He tossed away the pile of junk mail by the back door and put the shower curtain and the small throw rugs into the washing machine. Everything was organized and clean. But none of that made her feel any better.

On Tuesday Sila pulled up the shade and looked out the window for a train, but she saw only the empty track. It was the first day of the new school year. She had slept through the early caravan of freight cars.

Sila turned away, and her eyes fell on the bulletin board by the door. Her pictures of her mom and dad and old friends from school were there, but these were surrounded by so many new shots from the summer. There were photos of Veda. And of the flamingos. Sila had pictures of owls and hawks and hummingbirds. There were photos of the garden. The barn. Even the dung pile.

But the one picture she focused on was of herself with Mateo and Veda. Gio had taken the shot and printed it out for her. The two kids were standing by the pond with the elephant in the background. And the only one looking into the camera lens was Veda. Sila was wearing shorts, and her legs appeared to be solid muscle. That's what happens, she thought, when you push around a heavy wheelbarrow and ride a bicycle for two hours a day. She looked very tan in the picture but she knew it was mostly dust that came up off the road when they were biking. It stuck to her because she was sweating, and in the picture the terra-cotta color gave the impression that she was made of clay. She was laughing in the photo and her face looked joyous. Mateo's expression was serious, but his hands had been caught midair flapping, which she knew meant he was as happy as she was.

Sila got out of bed and went to her bureau to retrieve Mrs. Gardino's binder. She opened it and looked at what Gio's wife, once her teacher, had saved. She turned the pages slowly, stopping to look at the picture Mateo had drawn and then moving on until she got to the poem she'd written followed by "The sweetest little girl in the world." Sila exhaled. She was once sweet. But not anymore. Now she was, she decided, strong. It wasn't how the world saw her but how she saw herself that felt important.

Sila went into the kitchen, opened the cabinet under the sink, and pulled out her once-favorite shirt. Back in her room she was confused that the shirt was larger than she remembered. It hadn't grown in the last year. Had she shrunk? She stared at the fabric as if seeing it for the first time. The red, white, and blue was like a flag. There were no stars, but the bold colors said to her that she was, despite everything that had happened, an American. She loved where she lived and she wanted to be a part of her community.

She decided that she was going to wear it.

Sila was happy to see her friends Porter and Daisy and Nala, which surprised her. And what shocked her even more was that they were happy to see her. She hadn't realized that her old friends were a comfort until they surrounded her in the hall. Why had she stopped seeing these girls? How had they drifted out of her life over the past year? She didn't have much of an explanation. Things changed when her mother had gone overseas. Were they changing again? She was grateful that no one brought up the past. Today they were all starting anew as if she hadn't drifted away.

Was that what the summer was for?

Was it a way to press reset on life?

Four hours later, when the bell rang for lunch break, Sila's old friends seemed to appear out of nowhere to take up position at her elbows. They started down the wide hall moving toward the cafeteria as a group, the girls all talking at the same time. They were nearly at the entrance to the loud dining hall when Sila spotted Mateo. He was alone with a lunch bag in one hand and a book cradled to his chest in the other. She knew what was in that bag: a tuna fish sandwich, chips, and seven almonds. The book with the red cover in his other arm was about gravity.

Mateo had told her "the more massive the object, the greater the gravitational pull."

Gravity was why the planets circled the sun.

The spheres were pulled in and reaped the benefits of the warmth.

This past summer Gio had shown her a different planet.

Veda had been the kids' star.

Sila kept her eyes on Mateo. She thought he would never quit loving gravity. Did Mateo see her?

Sila turned to her old friends. "I'll meet you in the cafeteria." Porter reached out and caught hold of Sila's arm. "We'll just wait." But Sila shook her off gently. "No. See you in there. I'm going to be a while." The girls seemed to understand, and disappeared inside to eat as Sila made her way to Mateo.

"Hey, Mateo."

She wasn't surprised when he seemed startled to see her. He didn't smile. Before, that would have bothered her. Now it didn't.

"Do you want to eat lunch with me? We can sit in the cafeteria together. Either with some of the girls I used to hang out with or just the two of us by ourselves."

"I'm going to eat outside," Mateo said. "I like eating outdoors. It reminds me of being at Gio's. Plus it's too loud in there."

"Yeah. Good idea."

For a moment Mateo looked confused. "But I only have one sandwich."

"That's okay. I've got my own stuff for lunch." She held up a brown paper sack.

"Is yours tuna fish?" Mateo asked.

"Yes. Actually, it is."

The two kids found a spot on the steps just down from the double front doors of the main entrance. It was warm in the sun as Sila opened her paper sack and took out her sandwich. She knew that Mateo liked to eat in silence.

Sila closed her eyes and listened to the wind in the nearby maple trees. She made out the noise of street traffic, the roar of a motorcycle, and then the sound of a distant train, followed by two barking dogs. But all of that was interrupted when Mateo said, "I think your dad's here."

Sila opened her eyes to see her father's car slide to the curb.

Both the passenger's and the driver's side doors opened at the same time. Sila dropped her sandwich to the ground when she saw who it was that got out. Then she started to run. She didn't feel her feet on the ground as she raced down the walkway, over the grass, straight to the car.

She jumped into wide, outstretched arms, and the weight of her body knocked her mother against the car. Alp came around and tried to keep his daughter and wife upright as they stumbled to the grass laughing and crying.

Sila's mother was home.

And just like that the endless wait was over.

39.

The case of *Tekin vs. Grand Hotel Incorporated* went before the Oregon court fourteen months later, and in a unanimous decision the largest civil judgment in the state's history of labor dispute was awarded to Oya Tekin. She was given back pay for twenty-three months, and the right to return to her old job. But that wasn't what was so significant about the verdict. The Grand Hotel was found to have acted to punish her for pointing out their inequality in labor practices, and for that Oya was awarded damages. The amount of money was so high because it was determined that a senior employee of the hotel had made contact with immigration services in what was interpreted to be an attempt to have her deported.

Oya did not return to her job. Instead, she went to work for the Bureau of Labor and Industries as an advisor on employee rights. With the money from the settlement, the Tekins set up a college fund for their daughter. They pur-

chased a mechanic business for Alp. And they tried to buy an elephant.

It began with a train trip.

Sila and Mateo, accompanied by Oya, Alp, Rosa, and Gio, traveled for thirty-eight hours to Arizona, where they met the people who cared for Madhi, Veda's mother.

It took months of correspondence with the Randolf family who ran the sanctuary to make it happen. Sila believed that Veda needed to be with her mother. She pressed them endlessly to figure out how the two elephants could be together. Finally it was agreed that Sila and her parents, with Gio, Mateo, and Rosa, would make a trip to meet in person. And it was there that a deal was made.

Madhi would come live in Oregon at Gio's property, and when he was no longer alive, both elephants would return to Arizona, where the Randolf family would guarantee they would be properly looked after. There were still many details to work through, not the least of which was transporting the elephant to Oregon. But Madhi had spent most of her life in the circus, and she had traveled in trucks on highways for years.

Sila woke up and it was still dark outside. She was too excited to sleep. Six weeks had passed since the agreement had been made. She opened the window and stared out into the darkness, knowing that a train would pass soon. She could tell time by the freight cars and she knew that in four hours she would be driving out to Gio's. She had learned how to endure waiting, but it still felt as if her heart was going to explode.

Sila sat in the back seat with Mateo and his mother. Her parents were up front. When Alp pulled inside the gate at Gio's a hay truck was just leaving. A new, large order had been delivered, and Klay and Carlos were already working. There were bales stacked high on wooden pallets.

Sila took a seat on the steps next to Mateo to wait. Gio, Alp, Oya, and Rosa continued up to the porch to sit in the old wicker furniture. At 12:08 Mateo removed his lunch from his backpack and started eating his sandwich. Sila was too anxious to have any of the food they had brought. She watched the sky for birds, pointing out, "There are so many different species of birds out here."

"They're actually avian dinosaurs," Mateo clarified.

He finished chewing before telling her, "Life spread

around the world by the three W's: wind, wing, and water. The Hawaiian Islands are a good place to see this because they're late from an evolutionary perspective. The islands are all made from active volcanoes. The plants came from seeds carried by wind and birds. The ocean brought other life. But a lot of what you can see there today came from man."

Sila answered, "Maybe we'll go there one day."

Mateo had moved from his sandwich to his almonds. "First I'd like to see the North Pole. I'm interested in polar bears. Only, who isn't interested in polar bears?"

From behind them on the porch Gio chimed in, "Bears can be a bigger problem than you'd think."

Sila knew he was talking about Mr. Pickles.

They all heard the transporter before they saw it. Gio opened the gates and the large rig pulled in. There was an enormous covered crate on the back. Behind the flatbed was a second truck with a forklift.

A woman was driving the flatbed. She rolled down the window and called out: "Sila Tekin?"

The woman seemed surprised that a kid answered.

"I'm Sila."

"We've got your elephant."

The flatbed wheezed as it moved toward the barn. Then the rumbling engine shut down and the world fell silent. Sila could now hear her heart pounding in her ears. She was trying hard to stay calm. Maybe the biggest thing she had learned while her mother was away was how to wait. Patience truly did pay off.

Gio asked everyone to stay on the porch. Sila went up the steps and stood with her parents. Mateo leaned against the front door next to his mother. Luckily the view on the porch was good and Sila could see what was happening.

Once the trucks were in place, the forklift removed a metal platform from the flatbed and lowered it to the ground. It was a step for the elephant. Two men then untied the heavy tarp and pulled it off the metal enclosure.

Madhi was beautiful. She was bigger than Veda. Her skin was a stormy-sky color of gray, but the pigmentation around her ears and on most of her trunk was gone and she had big areas of pink hide everywhere else. It looked like she was a pink elephant with freckles.

Madhi knew to follow commands. First one rear foot stepped down out of the enclosure and then back onto the platform below, then the other. And then the front two. Once

Madhi was off the truck onto the ground, Sila could see that she had a big chain around the bottom of her front leg. Gio went over to the men and said something, and then one of them got a key and undid a lock. The metal links fell to the ground.

The sight of that happening made Sila's eyes fill up.

Klay and Carlos had gone down to the pond to be with Veda, and they'd placed watermelon, oranges, and bananas on the sandy shore. Gio checked in with them on his cell phone. Veda was eating at the water's edge.

Madhi had barely moved. The men had put four bales of hay in front of her, cutting the wire and spreading some of the straw out. The elephant looked interested, but didn't touch the stuff.

After the papers had been signed, the driver got into the cab of the flatbed and the two men helped her back the truck out the double set of gates. Their part of Madhi's journey was done and it wasn't long before they were gone.

Once the trucks were off the property, Madhi's trunk rose up high into the air. She was taking in the smells of this new world. She looked suddenly agitated. Her ears flared wide. She began to sway from side to side.

Gio got in the golf cart. "Get in, kids. Let's get Veda!"

Sila and Mateo climbed in the cart while their parents waited on the porch. Gio was usually careful about the potholes in the road, but not today. He was driving as fast as the "old bucket" could go. Sila gripped the aluminum frame that held up the cart's canopy and Mateo repeated multiple times, "We have a surprise for you, Veda."

Gio took his foot off the accelerator when they reached the top of the hill. It slowed to a stop as they looked down at Veda. Gio had trained her over the summer to come whenever he beeped the horn on the cart. He pressed down hard on the steering wheel, and Veda stared up with an expression that seemed to say, "What's going on?"

Sila couldn't stop herself from shouting, "Veda! You're not going to believe it!"

Gio honked the horn again, and Veda started out of the water. The flamingos swirled around her in their organized but confused way as she moved to the shore. Gio gave the horn another beep as he shouted, "Let's go, Veda! This way!"

She might have known it was the wrong time to go to the barn, but Veda was on the dirt road and heading up the hill. Gio put the golf cart in reverse and spun around in a big arc, still tooting the horn. Veda was halfway up the incline when her ears flared out wide and then her trunk shot up into the air. She started to walk faster. Sila knew that Asian elephants don't run. Only African elephants do that. But Veda was moving as quickly as Sila had ever seen. She was charging up the incline, her feet hitting the ground with such force that dust rose in puffs with each step.

Mateo's eyes were like lasers on the elephant. His voice was even as he said, "She knows."

Sila looked from Mateo to Gio, shouting, "Really?! Does she smell another elephant?"

Gio kept turning back to look at Veda. "I don't know!"

"What will she do when she sees Madhi?" Sila asked.

Mateo raised his voice. That was something he didn't do often. "We're about to find out!"

Up ahead on the road, moving straight toward the golf cart, was Madhi.

Gio yelled, "I really thought she'd stay with all that hay."

Madhi lifted her trunk and trumpeted. It was a big, long, incredibly loud blast. This happened just as Veda came up over the rise in the hill. The golf cart was on the road between Veda and Madhi, who were moving to each other like two cement trucks.

Veda's trunk rose up high into the air, and she answered the trumpeting with a blast of her own. Sila hadn't known she could make that kind of noise. Both elephants were moving fast. Then Gio did the only thing he could. He drove straight off the dirt road.

The golf cart bumped up and down as it rode over ferns and hit rocks. It grazed a tree, then when the left two wheels went up onto a rotten log they all screamed as the cart kept moving on an angle like a roller coaster car. Sila was certain they were going to flip. But luck was on their side and the cart thumped off the log and finally came to a stop a foot before a giant boulder.

They all looked back at the road just in time to see Veda and Madhi meet. Their trunks wrapped around each other. They both made loud rumbling noises that sounded to Sila like the largest cats in the world purring. They were rubbing up against each other in what seemed to be pure happiness.

They were lost from each other and then they were found.

They were back together after twenty-one years.

"Are you okay?" Gio asked the kids.

Sila nodded. Mateo took a while before saying, "I'm okay."

Sila couldn't take her eyes off the two elephants. She murmured, "I can't believe it."

And then she started to cry. Her tears were of joy. Of relief. Of fear. They were tears of gratitude. Of empathy.

Mateo looked over at his friend. "It's all right, Sila. I promise. It's okay."

She didn't know if he was talking about the two elephants, or just about everything in life. She didn't say anything. But her eyes said she believed him.

You had to hope for the best.

You had to keep going even when things weren't fair.

You had to believe in the possibility of days like this day.

And you had to work to make them happen.

40.

SHE WAS MY BABY, thought Madhi.

I WANTED TO KEEP HER SAFE.

BUT I COULDN'T STOP THEM

FROM TAKING HER AWAY.

AFTER THAT SHE WAS ONLY IN MY DREAMS.

UNTIL SO MUCH TIME PASSED

I WASN'T SURE SHE HAD EVER BEEN REAL.

I HAD ONLY ONE HOPE.

I SAID IT TO THE MOON AND THE SUN

AND THE OPEN SKY,

I SAID IT TO THE STARS.

MY ONLY WISH

TO THE WIND AND THE RAIN AND THE SNOW,

ONLY ONE THING IN THIS LIFE TO WANT,

AND THAT WAS TO SEE HER AGAIN.

TO KNOW SHE LIVED ON.

TO KNOW I WAS ONCE A MOTHER.

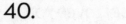

I DID NOT FORGET YOU, thought Veda.

BECAUSE I LOVED YOU.

AND BECAUSE I BELIEVED

THAT THERE WEREN'T JUST

BAD PEOPLE.

THERE WERE ALSO

GOOD PEOPLE

IN THIS WORLD.

I DID NOT FORGET YOU, MAMA

BECAUSE I BELIEVED IN OUR LOVE.

Acknowledgments

My editor and publisher at Dial, Lauri Hornik, cares about every single word. I am grateful for her incredible ideas, attention, and support. Lauri is a thoughtful person in all ways and I'm so fortunate to be able to work with her and the rest of the team at Penguin Random House, including Regina Castillo (copyeditor) and Rosanne Lauer (proofreader), Jessica Jenkins and Mina Chung (cover and interior designers), and Julie McLoughlin (cover artist).

Amy Berkower at Writers House, along with Cecilia de la Campa, are trusted advisers and wonderful friends.

I'm indebted to the help I received from Basak Agaoglu and Rabbi Ruti Regan, who both brought so much insight to this story.

When I was sixteen years old, I lived in Istanbul, Turkey and was a student at Robert Kolej (The American Robert College of Istanbul). The friendships made at that time changed my life. I want to particularly acknowledge Dilek Bulgu, Ayşen Keskin Zamanpur, Oya Göçmen Girit, Soli Özel, Herve Rijneveld, and Kate Thayer. Love to you all.

In my lifetime I haven't seen as much change as the world has experienced in this past year. School teachers and librarians remain my North Star.

The day starts and ends with Gary Rosen. Thank you more than anything, honey, for making me laugh.

Turn the page for an excerpt from

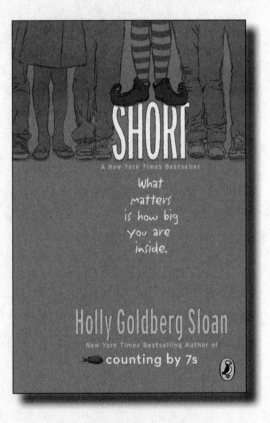

★ "Sweet and uplifting . . . [Julia's] self-acceptance is inspiring and the joy she experiences in her foray into theater is irresistible."   —*Booklist*, starred review

"Very funny . . . Theater kids and fans of Tim Federle's 'Nate' books will love this."   —*School Library Journal*

ONE

I spend a lot of time looking up.

My parents aren't short. My mom's even on the tall side. But my grandma Mittens (we really call her that) is tiny. I'm not good at science, but sometimes the genes from another generation sneak in and scramble the action. This might be to help you bond with the old people in your family.

One night when I was in the third grade I felt a sore throat coming on. I went down to ask for an aspirin or at least warm salt water to gargle. If there was a peanut butter cookie left on the dessert plate, I thought that might also help. My parents were hanging out in the living room, and I heard my father say, "Well, we're lucky Julia's a girl. What if she was a boy and that short?"

I stopped moving. They were talking about me.

I waited for my mom to say, "Come on, Glen, she's not *that* short!" But she didn't. She said, "Right? It's my mom's fault. Mittens did it to her." And then they both laughed.

Something had been done to me.

Like a crime.

It was someone's fault.

I know they love me like crazy, but I'm short and they aren't. Until that moment I didn't realize my size was a problem for them. Their words made a heavy feeling on my shoulders and I wasn't even wearing a bathrobe. It was like having sand in wet shoes or a knot of tangled hair that can't be combed through because there's gum in the middle. Plus part of their statement was sexist, which is also wrong.

I went back up to my room and didn't even ask for pain help. I climbed under the covers next to my dog, Ramon. He was asleep with his head on my pillow. When we first got him he was not allowed on the bed. But rules with dogs don't count in the same way as with people. I whispered in Ramon's ear, "I'm never going to say the word 'short' out loud again."

I didn't know how hard it would be. The word is everywhere.

These are the facts: In school I'm always in the front row for group pictures. None of the kids—even my best friends—want me on their team when we split up for basketball. I have a good shot, but it's too easy to block.

When we're on a family trip, I sit in the third seat, the one all the way in the rear. It's easier for me to curl up next to suitcases, plus I don't mind riding backward.

I need a stepstool to reach the water glasses in our kitchen, and I'm still small enough to fit through the dog door at home if we accidentally get locked out, which happens more often than you'd think.

Grandma Mittens calls me the family terrier. She says that terriers might be small dogs but they are also tough. I'm not sure if that's good or bad, because the only terrier I ever really knew was named Riptide, and he bit people.

Until seven weeks ago we had Ramon.

He wasn't a terrier.

He had black and white spots and was a mixed breed. Another way of describing him is to say he was a mutt. Only I don't like that word. It can have "negative connotations," which means it can come with bad thoughts. People think he was part pit bull because his head was big and he had a similar shape. But I don't want to label him.

We adopted Ramon from a rescue place that meets on Sundays in a parking lot next to the farmer's market. He was pretty much the best dog in the whole world. We had him for more than five years, and then only a month and a half ago he climbed up into my dad's chair in the living room (even though I don't know why it's called my dad's chair, because we all sit there, even the dog if no one is looking). Anyway, Ramon got up into the chair, which was the only place he wasn't supposed to sit. It was okay for him to be on the couch because we put a blanket there and it can be washed. But dad's chair is made of leather.

I came in and said, "Ramon, get down!"

He knew a lot of words, like "treat" and "sit" and "walk" and "squirrel" and "down," but that day he acted like he'd never heard a single sound in his life. His eyes kept looking straight ahead, and then his whole body sort of snapped. Like an electric shock happened.

We found out later he had heart disease. What happened in the chair was because of that.

Ramon died that night wrapped in my favorite green quilt at the vet's office.

We don't really know how old he was because of being adopted. What we do know is that we loved him with everything we have in us.

One thing that's still happening is that I'm looking all the time for Ramon. I walk into the living room and I expect to see him on the couch. Or maybe in the kitchen, where his favorite thing to do was sit on the little blue rug right in front of the refrigerator. Ramon's specialty was knowing how to get underfoot, but it was really that he figured out all the best places.

My grandma Mittens loves the obituaries, which is basically the dead people news. When she's visiting us she reads them aloud to me. I wish they had a pet section. It would be filled with interesting stories like:

LOCAL CAT DIES IN TWO-CAR CRASH

Or:

DOG WAS GREATEST BEAUTY OF HER TIME

Or maybe:

HAMSTER PIONEERED THEORY
ON EXERCISE

Maybe even:

NOTED GOLDFISH LEADER DIES UNDER
SUSPICIOUS CIRCUMSTANCES

Grandma Mittens read that headline to me when I was little and I've never forgotten. Only it wasn't about a goldfish. It was about a military leader in South America. I don't remember his name because I'm not good at storing historical facts.

One thing I've decided is that life is just one big, long struggle to find applause.

Even when people die, they are hoping someone writes a list of accomplishments about them.

Pets also like praise.

Well, maybe not cats, but I know whenever I said

"Good boy, Ramon!" he just filled up with happiness.

Ramon Marks's obituary would've read:

BEST DOG IN THE WORLD LEAVES BROKEN HEARTS AND AN EMPTY HOME

Since the night of the heart attack in the leather chair I've been trying to get over losing Ramon. My parents tell me: *Time heals all wounds.* But that's not actually true, because all kinds of things aren't healed by time. An example of this would be if you break your spinal cord in two, which means you would never walk again.

So I think what they mean is that one day the ache will feel not as achy.

The better expression might be: *Time has a way of making pain hurt less.*

That would be more accurate, but it's not my job to fix these kinds of sayings.

My school year ended ten days ago. I don't know why the school year and the regular year don't stop and start at the same time. The New Year starting on the first of January just seems all wrong. If they put me in charge, which no one ever has done, I'd make a year start on June 15 and I'd let kids off from school for two months to celebrate.

Now that school is finished, I'm hoping I can break free of feeling sad about Ramon, because it might be holding me back.

But I'm not going to forget Ramon.

Ever.

I asked for his collar, and I feel like my parents weren't that happy when I put it around the lamp right by my bed. If you look really close you can still spot his hairs stuck to the inside part. Also, it still smells like him.

It's not a great smell, but it's his smell, so that's what matters. I keep the metal name tag facing my pillow so I can see *RAMON* every morning when I wake up. It's important that I start my day by remembering him.

To be honest, I'm guessing *he* always started his day by thinking about his food bowl. He really loved to eat.

I'm the one who fed him.

I'm not saying that's why I was his favorite. But it was probably part of the reason.

Besides the collar I also have a small wooden carving that my uncle Jake made me. It looks just like Ramon.

Uncle Jake was once just a regular insurance salesman in Arizona living with Aunt Megan. One day they got in a car accident. Uncle Jake hurt his back and had to lie down in bed for a long time. Aunt Megan was worried he'd go crazy because he was a twitchy person, so she went to a craft shop and got him a whittling kit, which means carving stuff out of wood.

The first thing he made was called The Old Sea Captain. The kit gives you a block the size of your hand

and it's already in the right shape for the project. You just take the tool and carve away because they show you where to put the little knife by giving you a stencil. This isn't cheating. This is how you learn.

Uncle Jake went from doing The Old Sea Captain to all kinds of things that I guess were more complicated, and then he settled on carving birds. There are people who do this and enter contests, and he became one of those guys. He is now a world champion woodworker specializing in waterfowl.

It turns out that his secret talent is knowing how to very carefully move a sharp knife.

All of this happened before I was born, but he makes his money now carving sculptures instead of selling insurance.

Two and a half years ago he made me Ramon out of wood. I loved it then, but I really love it now.

Don't miss these novels by Holly Goldberg Sloan!

Counting by 7s

"Offbeat, and very touching—just like Willow herself." —*Entertainment Weekly*

★ "Poignant." —*The Horn Book*, starred

★ "[Willow's] journey of rebuilding the ties that unite people as a family will stay in readers' hearts long after the last page." —*School Library Journal*, starred

To Night Owl from Dogfish

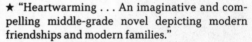

★ "Heartwarming . . . An imaginative and compelling middle-grade novel depicting modern friendships and modern families." —*School Library Journal*, starred review

"Laugh-out-loud . . . [Featuring] a dramatic climax and a host of surprising twists, the novel affirms that families conventional and unconventional are families just the same." —*Publishers Weekly*

Appleblossom the Possum

"A warm and funny possum-family saga." —*Kirkus Reviews*

"A perfectly sweet animal tale with just the right blend of humor, excitement, and uncertainty." —*School Library Journal*